All I know i̲s̲ ... before I even kne̲... something inside m̲... reason, all sense o̲... This was *war*.

"We'll get plenty of people to come to our talent show," I said, my voice oddly controlled. "In fact, it's going to be so packed that we'll be selling tickets for Standing Room Only."

"Yeah, right," Kicky said. "And what makes you think that's going to happen?"

The crowd was silent then. I could feel Wendy and Kicky's eyes burning into me. I was aware that beside me, Carla had grown stiff. All the kids who were looking on were strangely silent too, as if they were also dying to hear what I was about to say.

And then, as if it were actually someone else who was speaking, or at least controlling what words came out of my mouth, I heard myself say, "It just so happens that one of the acts in our talent show is going to be Johnny Rainbow."

WHAT DO ROCK STARS EAT FOR BREAKFAST?

Cynthia Blair

FAWCETT JUNIPER • NEW YORK

RLI: $\dfrac{\text{VL 5 \& up}}{\text{IL 6 \& up}}$

A Fawcett Juniper Book
Published by Ballantine Books
Copyright © 1993 by Cynthia Blair

Library of Congress Catalog Card Number: 93-90531

ISBN: 0-449-70413-0

Manufactured in the United States of America

First Edition: November 1993

chapter
one

Once upon a time—isn't that a good way to start?—there were three girls named Betsy, Samantha, and Carla, who were the best of friends. They were such good friends, in fact, that they even picked a name for themselves: the Bubble Gum Gang. But the funny thing was, the one who had pretty much come up with the idea of the Bubble Gum Gang, the one who you could even say had *created* the Bubble Gum Gang in the first place, turned out to be the one who almost made it fall apart.

Sounds pretty crazy, huh? Yet that's exactly what happened. The girl I'm talking about just happens to be me, Betsy Crane. Yes, I'm the guilty one. I'm the one who came *this* close to taking the very best thing that had ever happened to me . . . and screwing it all up.

Oddly enough, it all started the day that Carla, Samantha, and I found ourselves standing in front of our first-period English class, giving a report on the theme of friendship in literature.

"And that's the story of Damon and Pythias," I said, nervously running my fingers through the wild mane of reddish curls that calls itself my hair. "These two characters from Greek myths have symbolized friendship for thousands of years."

It was almost over. And boy, was I ever relieved. I had been dreading this presentation for days. Weeks, even. You see, one of my least favorite things in the entire world is standing up and talking in front of a group of people. That's what happens when you're as shy as I am. Even giving an oral report in a silly old English class becomes a reason for major butterfly-in-the-stomach activity. The fact that the audience was mostly guys staring out the window and girls passing notes back and forth hardly helped at all.

"Okay," I said, starting to feel almost like a normal person once again now that my part of the report was just about done. "If there aren't any questions about Damon and Pythias, then Carla will give her report on—"

"I have a question." Way in the back corner of the room, a long arm shot up into the air. That arm, I quickly figured out, belonged to Skip Jones, one of my least favorite people in my English class, if not in the entire galaxy.

"Yes?" I asked. I tried to sound pleasant. But I was thinking, *Now* what?

Skip, one of those tall, husky types whose jeans always look as if they're about to slide off, had this annoying smirk on his face. In fact, it's the exact same smirk he wore about ninety-nine percent of the time. He wore it whenever one of his teachers was chewing him out. Or even the school principal, Ms. Trayton.

"These two guys," he said, "this Damien and Percy, or whatever their names were. . . ."

"Damon and Pythias." I was trying my hardest to be patient.

"Whoever. If they lived such a long time ago, and there were no books or video tapes or anything back in ancient Greece, then how come we still know about them? I mean, Ray here is my best buddy, and I don't expect people to be doing reports on us in the year 3000."

Just then Ray Hutchinson leaned over and slapped Skip on the back. "Way to go, Skip, my man."

It took everything I had not to stick my tongue out at those two. Honestly, the way some people go out of their way to make trouble. Especially for those of us who are having a hard enough time just getting through the oral reports that certain teachers seem to love using to torture their students.

"Well, Skip," I began, "there are a lot of Greek myths that have been passed down through the ages. This is just one of them that—"

"Yeah, but *how*? You're not answering my question." He was still grinning, but from his tone of voice it sounded more like he was trying to start a fist fight than catch up on ancient history.

Still, I *was* supposed to be the expert. "Uh, I guess that, uh . . ."

Thank goodness for English teachers. Mr. Homer, not exactly the most on-top-of-things guy in the world, jumped in to save the day.

"Mr. Jones," he said from the opposite corner in the back of the classroom, "why don't we save that discussion for another day? Right now, I think we're all anxious to hear Carla's portion of the presentation."

I sat down in one of the three chairs that we had set up in front of the room, facing the class. Never had an orange molded piece of plastic felt so good.

I glanced over at Samantha, sitting right next to me.

"Great job," she whispered, giving me a huge, warm smile.

Carla, still getting her notes together, heard us and looked over her shoulder at me. "Yeah, Betsy. You were terrific."

As I sat there listening to Carla Farrell talk about Mark Twain's famous set of friends, Tom Sawyer and Huckleberry Finn, I found my mind wandering. Not that Carla's speech wasn't first-rate; it was. It's just that I couldn't help thinking about how this whole thing had come about. The three of us giving a presentation on friendship, that is.

The way it got started was that a few weeks earlier—right at the beginning of the school year, in fact—Mr. Homer had gotten this brainstorm. He assigned a group project. The idea was to pick a theme that commonly occurs in literature, and then do a whole bunch of assignments on that theme: book reports, a big end-of-the-semester term paper . . . and an oral presentation.

My first reaction, back during that first week of school, was to be about as excited as the time my dentist told me that there were probably going to be braces in my future. You see, I've always been pretty much of a loner, preferring to do my homework by myself. But there I was, grouped together with two other girls, without a whole lot of choice in the matter.

Our first mission was to choose a topic. That one took us a while. But by the time we had solved our first mystery together, nicknamed our threesome the "Bubble Gum Gang," and started on the road to a wonderful friendship, choosing a topic was a piece of cake.

Let me explain the part about calling ourselves the Bubble Gum Gang—aside from the fact that chewing gum is something we all love. Sure, we're pals. Even more than that, we're dedicated to seeking adventure and solving mysteries—every time one pops up in our hometown of Hanover, that is. But it's not as if the Bubble Gum Gang is a club. Actually, it's a whole lot more complicated than that.

Back in the old days, before the three of us became friends, we were all kind of what you'd call social misfits. Take me, for example. I've always had a problem with being labeled the "class brain" or "teacher's pet" or even, on occasion, a "nerd." That's what happens when you're someone who's smart enough to learn things a little more quickly than everybody else in the class. Not that I ever tried to make a big deal about it. Even so, somehow people just drew their own conclusions about me . . . without ever taking the time to find out if they were right or not.

Carla, meanwhile, has always been overweight. All her life, just about, there was always some clown around who insisted on making fun of "the fat girl." That meant the *other* kids were afraid of acting too friendly, in case they might end up getting made fun of too. . . . So Carla Farrell kept to herself, trying to hide behind baggy clothes that did little to bring out her short, dark, curly hair or her dark eyes or her pretty features.

Anyway, shortly after the Bubble Gum Gang was formed, she started on a brand-new diet. And this time, she was determined to stick with it. That was partly because she was tired of being the chubbiest girl in the class. It was also partly because she realized that giving in to her passion for eating was getting in the way of her other passion in life, acting. And it was partly because she now had two good friends to stick by her, helping her switch to a healthier way of eating.

Samantha, meanwhile, had an entirely different reason for being singled out as "different" by the other kids at school. She happened to be a member of what was easily the wealthiest family in all of Hanover. The Langtrees lived in the biggest house in town, drove the fanciest cars, and took the most exotic vacations.

Even though Samantha was only twelve years old, like Carla and me, she had already traveled all over the world. Just that past summer, for example, she and her parents and her two sisters had toured Europe, visiting eight different countries. A far cry from the five days at Disney World that most of us considered the ultimate vacation!

The way Sam looked made her stand out from the rest of the kids, too. And it wasn't even her long blond hair, her sparkling blue eyes, and the graceful way she carried herself. It was more the way she dressed, in fashions that were years ahead of what anybody in Hanover was wearing. What would you expect, when she got most of her clothes from stylish boutiques in Paris, London, and Milan?

Samantha was one of the nicest, sweetest, most caring people I have ever met. Yet because she was from such a rich family, the other kids just assumed she was a snob. That meant she ended up being an outcast, too.

Anyway, after a lifetime of being on the outside, each of us for a very different reason, we were glad to have finally formed a group of our own. We were friends. We were pals. We were the Bubble Gum Gang.

"And so," Carla said, sounding ready to wrap things up, "the friendship of Mark Twain's best-known characters, Tom Sawyer and Huckleberry Finn, is one of the finest examples we have of the theme of friendship in literature."

Our time was just about up. It was time for me to speak again—this time, to give a summary. But I was going to do even more than simply say a few inspiring words that would drive the other members of my English class to race right up to the school library the very first chance they got, demanding copies of *Huckleberry Finn*.

As a matter of fact, I was planning a surprise. And the ones who would be the most surprised were not the other members of the class. Not Mr. Homer, either. The people the surprise was for were none other than Carla Farrell and Samantha Langtree.

"At first, when Carla and Sam and I started researching this project," I began, "I didn't really get how studying something like friendship had anything to do with me. But by the time the three of us finished writing this report, I had really come to understand why having friends is so important.

"When I first moved to Hanover, just a couple of months ago, I was convinced I'd never make a single friend here. I was all set to be labeled 'the new girl' . . . probably for the rest of my life. But then I found Carla and Samantha, the two best friends anybody could ever have."

I glanced over at the two of them. Carla was turning as red as the bright crimson sweater she happened to be wearing that day. Samantha, meanwhile, looked as if she were about to burst into tears.

"We became such good friends so quickly, in fact, that we even picked a name. We call ourselves the Bubble Gum Gang."

None of this was a surprise to Sam or Carla, of course. But I had a little trick up my sleeve—or in my book bag, to be more accurate.

"Carla and Samantha didn't know it," I went on, "but every time I had a piece of bubble gum since the beginning of the year, I saved the paper wrapper. And as a tribute to our friendship, I wove the wrappers into a chain."

With great drama, I reached into my green canvas book bag, which was lying across my desk in the front of the room. I felt like one of those magicians I'm always seeing on TV. I pulled out the bubble gum chain, already almost three feet long.

"Here it is!" I announced proudly, holding it up like a long paper streamer. It was pretty, I had to admit, a white chain dotted with bright colors. "A tribute to the Bubble Gum Gang. The longer this thing gets, the deeper our friendship will become."

Shyly, I looked over at my two friends again, anxious to see how they were reacting. Carla was no longer red. Instead, she was wearing this huge, sloppy grin that was making her look as if she were about to burst. As for Samantha, those tears that had been threatening to fall before were now streaming down her face.

I turned back to the class. For a second, I had forgotten they were there. I saw that Skip and Ray looked as if they were about to explode into hysterical laughter. But at that moment, I couldn't have cared less.

Mr. Homer was smiling as he came up to the front of the room.

"Very nice job, girls," he said, nodding furiously. The way his head was bobbing up and down reminded me of a balloon. "Excellent. Excellent."

"I guess *they* got an *A*," one of the girls in the front of the room said to the boy next to her.

I knew she was probably right. But do you know what? At that moment, the grade we were going to get on our report didn't matter one bit.

The three of us were still feeling pretty good about the way our oral report had gone when the last bell rang.

"I don't know if I'm happy or sad to be bringing these books back," Samantha moaned when the three of us met at the school library right after school.

"I know exactly what you mean," Carla agreed. "Working on this project together has been so much fun." She was clutching her Mark Twain books, acting as if somebody was going to have to pry them away from her, finger by finger.

"Come on, you two," I insisted, slinging my green

canvas book bag over my shoulder. "Sure, this report on friendship was fun. But it's not as if we're not going to work together on any other projects. I mean, we're talking about the Bubble Gum Gang here, remember? The group that's committed to unraveling mysteries? Uncovering secrets? Solving puzzles?"

"Good point." Carla had already plopped her books onto the front counter. "Who knows where we'll go from here?"

"Right," I replied. Grinning, I added, "After all, remember what the bubble gum chain means. The longer we're friends, the longer it grows."

"*Sh-h-h-h!*" somebody hissed loudly, causing us all to jump.

I whirled around and saw that Mr. Pease, the school librarian, had just come out of his office.

"Girls!" the tiny bald-headed man cried in a loud, hoarse whisper. He was peering at us from behind the thick tortoiseshell glasses that were always slipping down his nose. "Keep your voices down, please!"

I was tempted to point out that he was making more noise than any of us.

"This is a library. A place of reading. Of thinking. Of serious contemplation."

I glanced around the library. True, it was a nice-looking room. It was large and airy, with thick blue carpeting everywhere, even Mr. Pease's office. But serious contemplation? In one corner, over at the computers, an eighth-grade boy was playing Earth Invaders. In back were a few ninth-grade girls poring over the latest issue of a fashion magazine. A couple of other kids were sitting at the largest table playing tic-tac-toe.

But Sam and Carla and I slunk away to a corner, continuing our conversation in a whisper.

"I suppose it's a relief that the project is over, especially since there are turkeys like Skip and Ray in our class who just love to make trouble." Carla sank into one of the soft, padded chairs that was perfect for curling up with a good book—or a fast-paced game of tic-tac-toe, depending on your taste. "Now I can start worrying about the *next* major event in my life."

"The school play," Samantha said with a grin. "If *I* were the one who was going to be in the opening of *Our Town* tomorrow night, that's all I'd be able to think about, oral report or no oral report."

"Me, too," I agreed. "I can't even imagine going on stage in front of an auditorium full of people. Doing it in Mr. Homer's class was bad enough."

Carla just shrugged. "I always get nervous right before I go on. But it goes away. Once you're out there, on the stage. . . ."

Her voice had become dreamy, and her eyes had that faraway look they always got whenever she talked about acting.

"Anyway," she went on, snapping back into reality, "tonight's the dress rehearsal. It's our last chance to run through the whole performance, from start to finish, before opening night. For me, that's always one of the most exciting parts of being in a play. You get to see how the whole thing fits together, knowing that the next time you do it, you'll be sharing the experience with the audience. . . ."

I was about to tell her how proud I was of her, and how I could hardly wait to see the Drama Club's production of Thornton Wilder's famous play, when there was a commotion at the library's main entrance. I looked up—and wasn't at all surprised to see who it was that was making such a dramatic entrance.

Wendy Lipton and Kicky Blake, two of the school's most popular girls, were standing in the doorway, looking as if they were posing for the fashion magazine those ninth-grade girls were reading. And it was obvious why. They were both wearing the brand-new sweaters that, as they had already told nine-tenths of the school, were being considered as part of the cheerleaders' new uniforms. Since Wendy was the head cheerleader, and Kicky was her unofficial assistant, it was up to them to make the final decision. And so for the past few days, everywhere they went, they wore identical white cardigans, trimmed in the school's colors, orange and black. On the left side was an appliquéd tiger, Hanover Junior High School's mascot.

"Uh, oh," I muttered. "Here comes trouble."

While Wendy and Kicky were not exactly what you'd call the friendliest girls around, they seemed to have taken a particular dislike to the members of the Bubble Gum Gang. One reason is that girls like *them* consider girls like *us* unworthy of the air we breathe. That's mainly because we're not stuck-up cheerleaders whose idea of a good time is having contests to see who can get more boys to ask them to the next school dance.

A second reason is that earlier that fall, Wendy and Carla went after the same part in *Our Town*. There's a third reason, too—as if the first two weren't already enough. A few weeks before, Wendy and Kicky and the rest of their crowd had tried to lure Samantha into their little clique, for reasons that were anything but friendly. They hadn't exactly been thrilled by her rejection.

At any rate, all three of us had come to expect the worst from Wendy and Kicky. And from the way their expressions changed the moment they spotted us huddled together in the corner of the library, I knew immediately that "the worst" was precisely what we were about to get.

"Oh, *hi*, Betsy," Kicky cooed, nudging her friend in the side with her elbow. "Hi, Samantha. Hi, Carla."

We all mumbled something that sounded sort of like a greeting.

"Let's just *run*," I suggested in a low voice.

But it was too late. Kicky and Wendy were already making a beeline in our direction.

"Hi-i-i," cried Wendy. "How do you like our new sweaters? Aren't they the most awesome things you've ever seen in your life?"

She came over, flicking her long blond hair over her shoulder, and stood right smack in front of us. It was as if we were supposed to feel privileged or something, just for having the opportunity to admire her stupid sweater.

"Very nice," Samantha said politely. She reached over and stroked the hem. "It's quite soft."

"Oh, yes. That's because it has angora in it. I just love fuzzy sweaters, don't you?"

"Not if they have tigers on them," Carla remarked.

Wendy's sugary-sweet smile faded. "Well, of course angora sweaters *never* look good on fat girls."

I could feel the fury rising inside me. It was all I could do to keep from ripping that sweater off that creepy Wendy then and there. Samantha must have sensed that, because she gently placed her hand on my arm. I glanced over at Carla, almost afraid to see how she was reacting. But she just laughed.

"Poor Wendy," she said. "I can only feel sorry for a girl who thinks a ridiculous sweater is the most important thing in the world."

Wendy's eyes flashed angrily. "Oh, really? And what do you think is important, Carla? Friendship? Stupid chains made out of old gum wrappers? I think that's taking this recycling thing just a little bit too far."

Kicky giggled. "That's a good one, Wendy. You're so clever sometimes."

But Wendy hardly seemed to have heard her. "You

know, all the kids in Mr. Homer's first-period English class are talking about how the three of you made total fools of yourselves this morning. All that soppy stuff about friendship and gum wrapper chains and calling yourselves the Bubble Gum Gang. . . . If *I* were doing such babyish things, *I'd* keep them to myself!''

Samantha took a step forward. "Be careful, Wendy. You're really stepping out of bounds here.''

Carla gripped my arm. "Come on, Betsy. Let's just get out of here.''

"I heard Skip and Ray laughing about it,'' Wendy went on in this wheedling tone. "In fact, they're going around telling the whole school about it! I mean, come on, Samantha. Crying, right in front of your whole English class? I guess some people would do anything to get an *A*.''

Samantha glanced at me. "I think we've all had enough.''

With that, I grabbed my book bag and my jacket and stalked out of the library. And my two friends were right behind me.

chapter
two

"The way those two act, you'd think they were *princesses* or something!" I exclaimed as Samantha and Carla and I walked home from school together that same afternoon.

Carla shook her head. "Princesses would never act like that. They would know better."

"Don't waste your time worrying about Kicky and Wendy," said Samantha. "They don't deserve the space they're taking up in your brain."

I was about to tell Samantha that she was absolutely right when I suddenly stopped dead in my tracks.

"What on *earth*?"

All thoughts of Wendy and Kicky and angora sweaters with tigers on them vanished. I simply stared, not quite able to believe what I was seeing. But those two green orbs that had done so well by me for the entire twelve years of my life—green orbs better known as my eyes—weren't lying.

"What is it?" Carla demanded. By this point, she, too, had stopped walking.

"Is everything all right?" asked Samantha, frowning. Like Carla, she was looking around, trying to figure out what had caused me to gasp.

"Look at the elementary school playground!" I cried, pointing at the fenced-in area half-hidden behind some trees. "It looks like it got hit by an earthquake!"

I wasn't exaggerating, either. The playground equipment had been ripped out of the ground. Both swing sets were lying on their sides, and the supports on the slide had been pulled out of the grassy schoolyard. There was also one of those merry-go-round things that's propelled by little kids' sneakers digging into the soft dirt all around it. It was half-dismantled, with the round wooden platform separated from the base.

Standing in the middle of all the wreckage was a truck that was a cross between a crane and a tractor. It looked mean, as if it had actually enjoyed the damage it had already done . . . and in fact could hardly wait to do more.

By that point Samantha and Carla were both looking in the direction in which I was staring. It only took a few seconds before their mouths dropped open just like mine. The three of us would have looked pretty weird to anyone who walked by and saw us. But that's hardly the kind of thing we were thinking about.

"Come on. Let's get a better look," I suggested. It was just a short walk through the trees to the edge of the playground.

"What do you suppose is going on?" asked Carla in amazement. "Why would anybody take apart a playground?"

"Where are the children going to play?" Samantha had put down her schoolbooks and grabbed hold of the chain-link fence. Her face was pressed against the metal.

"It looks just awful," I added. "What an eye-sore!"

"Look at that lock." Carla used her chin to gesture toward the huge chain wrapped around the gate, fastened with a metal lock about as big as my math textbook. "That is one serious lock."

"Look at that *sign*," said Samantha. "KEEP OUT! PLAYGROUND CLOSED UNTIL FURTHER NOTICE!" She gave a little shudder.

We were all silent for a long time.

"You know," Carla finally said in a soft voice, "Sam and I both went to this school. And one of my very best memories is playing on that playground after lunch every day. I would go on the swings and pump as hard as I could, pretending I could fly. . . ."

"The slide was always my favorite," Samantha remembered wistfully. "I would go on it over and over and over again. I never got tired of it."

"Maybe . . ." Samantha said, "maybe this isn't what we think it is. It could be that they've simply decided to redo the whole thing. You know, plant some more grass, get brand-new playground equipment. . . ."

"Maybe they'll even plant some flowers around the edge," Carla suggested, sounding hopeful. "That would make the kids' playground really pretty."

"I hope they put in some really high slides," said Samantha. "Those were always my favorite."

I just looked at them. "All that sounds just fine and dandy, but what if you're both wrong?"

Carla and Samatha stared back at me.

"What do you mean, Betsy?" Carla demanded. "I didn't really mean it about the flowers along the edges, you know. I realize that a couple of frisbees gone out of control and those flowers would be history."

"No, no," I said impatiently. "I mean maybe they're not redoing the playground. Maybe they're just . . . I don't know, taking it away."

"They wouldn't do that!" Samantha cried. Then, in a softer voice, she added, "Would they?"

"Maybe they're planning to build another shopping center here," Carla said, narrowing her eyes. "You know how you go to bed one night and everything is the same as always, and you wake up the next morning and there's this string of eight brand-new stores that you never saw before?"

"I hope not!" Samantha wailed. "Those school-children need a playground!"

"Well, you know what they say," I said firmly. "There's only one way to find out."

Carla looked at me, blinking. "And what's that, Betsy?"

"Why, go find the elementary school principal and ask!"

Carla and Samantha responded exactly the way I expected they would. They thought for about a sixteenth of a second, picked up their school books, and then followed me into the school.

"Ms. Franklin will see you now," said the secretary sitting behind the desk in the elementary school's main office.

Carla, Sam, and I looked up, blinking. It felt kind of funny, sitting in the principal's office, waiting to see Ms. Franklin. What made it so weird was that instead of being there because we were in trouble, like most kids who found themselves in that situation, we were being treated as if we were grown-up.

I wasn't the only one who noticed, either.

"Gee, this feels funny," Carla giggled. "I haven't been back inside this school building since last spring, when I graduated from the sixth grade. Back then, this place felt like my second home. But now that I'm coming back as a seventh grader, everything seems so strange!"

"I know," Samantha agreed, her voice nearly a whisper. "I keep noticing how *little* everything looks. The water fountains in the hallways are so low. That's not at all the way I remember them. You practically have to kneel on the floor to get a drink! And did you happen to notice how tiny the chairs and the desks in the first-grade room are? They look like dollhouse furniture!''

What was most surprising, though, was the way Ms. Franklin, the principal of Hanover Elementary School, acted toward us. As she came out of her office, she was wearing a big smile and holding out her hand. While I had never actually gone to that school, it still felt weird, having a principal treat me this way.

"Hello, Carla. How are you?'' she said warmly, shaking Carla's hand. "And Samantha, how lovely it is to see you again.''

My two friends had suddenly become shy. Samantha's cheeks had turned a bright shade of pink, and Carla was staring at her shoes as if they were the most fascinating thing she had ever seen in her life. Somebody had to say *something*. And I was realizing fast that that somebody was going to have to be me.

"Hello, Ms. Franklin,'' I said boldly. "My name is Betsy Crane. I just moved to Hanover this summer, so I never went to this school.''

"Hello, Betsy.'' Ms. Franklin smiled, then shook my hand. "Why don't you three girls come into my office? My secretary tells me there's something troubling you. I hope I can help you out.''

I felt really important as I sat down opposite Ms. Franklin, who had just settled in comfortably behind her big desk. Carla was on my right and Samantha was on my left. But since they both still looked as if they were in awe of the whole situation, I got the feeling that I was unofficially in charge.

"The reason we're here is that we were curious about what happened to the school playground," I began, folding my hands neatly in my lap. "We noticed as we were walking home from school just now that it's been all ripped apart."

"Where are the children supposed to play?" Carla piped up.

"Are you planning to build a new one?" Samantha asked at the same time.

Ms. Franklin shook her head sadly. "I wish I could report that we were simply renovating that old playground. But I'm afraid that the news isn't quite that good."

The school principal stood up and went over to the window. From where she was standing, she could see the rusty old playground equipment, half out of the ground, and the mean-looking truck that had been responsible.

At that moment I took a good look at her. She was about my mother's age, I saw, a rather pretty woman with straight brown hair cut at her chin. She was dressed in a serious-looking dark blue suit that was softened only by the pretty flowered silk scarf tied at her neck. But instead of looking like a stern, no-nonsense principal, at the moment she looked like a woman who was very, very sad.

"You see," she went on, "last week some people from the state came to inspect the playground. We expected it to be nothing more than a routine visit. But when they saw how rusty and outdated our equipment was, they declared it unsafe. They insisted that we close down the playground immediately. They even demanded that we get the slides and the swings and the merry-go-round off the premises as soon as possible, to avoid the possibility of any children sneaking in and getting hurt.''

She looked back at us and said softly, ''By the end of next week, that playground will be nothing more than a vacant lot. Oh, of course the children will still be able to run around there. They can play tag and baseball and jump rope . . . but somehow, it just won't be the same.''

''It sure won't!'' Carla cried. ''Sam and I were just talking about how much we loved playing on that playground when we went to this school.''

Samantha was nodding. ''Right after lunch, every single day. I could hardly wait to get out there and go on that slide!''

''But what about rebuilding the playground?'' I suggested. ''Once all the outdated equipment is out of the way, can't the school simply put in new swing sets and slides?''

Ms. Franklin sat down at her desk again. Actually, it was more like she sank into her chair. Even though she had seemed pretty energetic to me, all of a sudden she looked tired.

''I wish we could,'' she said with a sigh. ''But

there simply isn't enough money in the school budget to buy any new equipment. I'm afraid that for now, the children of Hanover Elementary School are just going to have to do without a playground."

chapter
three

"Every time I think of those poor little kids with no playground," Samantha said sadly, "I feel like crying."

"I know," I agreed. "Something this serious sure makes our little scene at the school library with Wendy and Kicky seem silly."

It was later that same day, and the three of us were sitting around the kitchen table at my house. Actually, calling it a house isn't quite correct; it's more like an apartment. A garden apartment. The summer before, right after my parents decided to get divorced, my mom, my younger brother Brad, and I all moved to Clifton Garden Homes. At first, it took some getting used to, living in this super-modern complex where everything—the carpeting, the kitchen appliances, even the doorknobs—looked as if they were about two hours old. But by now, after only three short months, it was home.

Anyway, there we were, having one of our powwows after school. We were snacking on popcorn, warm and fresh and right out of the microwave. I mentioned before that Carla had recently started a brand-new diet, and that Sam and I were doing what we could to help her. Part of that meant eating the same healthy foods she was eating. And believe it or not, popcorn is one of the best things for you. Without the butter and the salt, that is.

"I just wish there were something we could do," Samantha went on, distractedly placing popcorn in her mouth, one kernel at a time.

I've always figured it was the fact that she has traveled in Europe, probably having dinner with queens and barons for all I know, that helped her develop such incredible manners. Every time I sat at a table and ate with her, I felt like I was taking a class at some fancy finishing school.

"I loved that playground," she went on. "And it breaks my heart to think that the other kids who are going to Hanover Elementary School now aren't going to be able to enjoy it the way I did."

"I know," I said, nodding. "I can't stop thinking about it, either. Boy, if only there were something we could do."

"It would cost a fortune to build a brand-new school playground," said Samantha. "Where would we ever get that much money?"

"If only there were some way we could raise the money," I said, thinking aloud.

Samantha brightened. "Maybe we could go around

from house to house, asking people to make dona-
tions. I'm sure my father would be willing to chip in.
I bet a lot of people who live in Hanover would love
to help out.''

''That's not a bad idea,'' I said. ''Or we could get
creative and hold a bake sale. . . .''

''Or a fair,'' Sam suggested.

''There's always a car wash.''

Yes, they were all good ideas. But none of them
were *great* ideas. Bake sales and fairs and car washes
had all been done before. Hardly the kind of thing
anyone was likely to get excited about. Besides, how
much money could you actually raise, selling home-
made cupcakes with pink icing and sprinkles, or hos-
ing down Fords and Toyotas? If we really wanted to
raise enough money to build a brand-new playground,
we were going to have to come up with something
better than that.

''Do you have any ideas, Carla?'' I asked, not
wanting her to feel left out of the conversation. So
far, I had noticed, she hadn't said very much.

''Hmmm?'' Carla glanced up from her popcorn,
looking as if she had been about eighteen thousand
miles away. ''Oh, I'm sorry, Betsy. What were you
saying?''

Samantha and I looked at each other and then burst
out laughing.

''Earth to Carla, Earth to Carla,'' I said between
giggles. ''Carla Farrell, where are you?''

She turned pink as she explained, ''I'm afraid I'm

not very good company today. All I can think about is the fact that the play is opening tomorrow night. I sure hope tonight's dress rehearsal goes well.''

''Why shouldn't it?'' asked Samantha, always the optimist.

But Carla didn't seem to have heard her. ''I keep picturing myself up there on stage, performing *Our Town* in front of a real live audience. . . . Breathing, thinking, ticket-buying people . . . And tonight is our last chance to polish it up. We'll be in full costume— not that there's much in the way of costumes. Scenery, either. The whole production is very simple, exactly the way it was intended to be. Still, there are so many things that can go wrong. . . .''

''Well, I know one thing that's not going to go wrong,'' I said firmly.

Carla looked puzzled. ''What's that?''

''Your performance, that's what! Carla, there's absolutely no question in my mind that you are going to steal the show. It's guaranteed!''

''Betsy's right,'' said Samantha. ''You're going to be terrific. And I, for one, can hardly wait for tomorrow night. Why, you've been rehearsing this play for weeks! And you've been telling us so much about it that I'm practically counting the minutes until curtain time.''

''Thanks,'' Carla said gratefully. ''I'll be thinking about you two, sitting out there with my eighty-nine relatives.'' She sighed, then said, ''I just wish I weren't so nervous.''

"That's natural," I assured her. "I'm sure everybody in the entire cast is nervous."

"Everybody except Wendy." Carla made a face. "Even though she's got such an important part in the play, she's been acting as if it's no more important to her than . . . than deciding which cheer to start cheerleading practice with!"

She shook her head slowly. "Speaking of Wendy, I just hope she does okay tomorrow night. I'm so afraid she's going to mess it up. I can picture her ruining the whole thing!"

"If she does a bad job," Samantha insisted, "she'll only make herself look bad. It will have nothing to do with the other members of the Drama Club. Just make sure you do as good a job as you can when you're up on stage playing your role."

"Speaking of playing roles," I said, "I'm supposed to be playing the role of hostess here. How about something to drink?"

"That sounds nice," said Samantha.

"I think there's some orange juice in the refrigerator. Unless Brad inhaled it all at breakfast this morning."

As I stood up to check, I noticed something I hadn't seen before. On the kitchen counter was the latest copy of *Rockers 'n' Rollers* magazine. It was not the kind of thing I usually read; being an egghead by nature, I lean toward books that have more words than pictures in them.

But before I spent too much time trying to figure

out what it was doing there, I noticed that there was a note on the front of the magazine. It was stuck right smack in the middle of the face of some rock star—who, I had to admit, was not at all bad-looking. The note was from my mom.

"Betsy," she had written, "a woman at work, whose husband works for a magazine company, gave me this. She knew I had a twelve-year-old daughter, and she thought you might enjoy it."

"Look at this," I muttered, picking it up. "I guess Mom left it here before she went to work this morning. Somebody at her job gave it to her."

"How is your mother's new job?" asked Samantha.

But before I had a chance to answer her, Carla pounced.

"Oh, *wow*!" she cried, jumping out of her chair—nearly knocking it over, in fact. "That's Johnny Rainbow on the cover! Isn't he the cutest guy you've ever seen in your life?"

"Johnny Rainbow?" I repeated, blinking. "Who's he?"

"Who's *he*?" Carla sounded as amazed as if I had just told her I was secretly from another planet.

"I've heard of him," Samantha volunteered. "He's a singer who just burst onto the music scene recently, right? All the magazines are writing about him."

"Johnny Rainbow," Carla squealed, "is simply the dreamiest thing to have ever walked the face of the earth. Please, please, *please* let me see that, Betsy!"

I was shocked by her reaction. Just two minutes earlier this girl had been moaning about how she could think of nothing but the play she was going to be in. Now, her eyes were bright, and she was wearing a big, moony grin. All because of a rock singer named Johnny Rainbow.

"Boy, I'd better check this guy out," I muttered.

But Carla acted as if she hadn't heard me. "I have every single one of his albums," she said, flipping through the magazine. "Of course, he only has two out so far, but I have them both. I've listened to them so many times that I know every single word of every single song."

She let out a yelp. "Oh, wow! Here are more pictures of him! And look, a long article! I *have* to read it, this very instant."

Samantha and I looked at each other again. This time, we just shrugged.

"Gee," I said, shaking my head. "And here I thought I knew everything there was to know about my pal Carla Farrell."

"A secret life," Samantha concluded with a big grin.

"Oooh, look!" Carla was still glued to her magazine. "Here's a section listing all of Johnny Rainbow's favorites."

"Oh, boy," I breathed. "I can hardly wait to hear." I got up to get some of that orange juice. Fortunately, my little brother, the human food-consuming machine, had left some in the container. He must have been running late.

Carla began to read aloud. "Johnny's favorite color is turquoise blue. That's *my* favorite color, too! Do you believe it?"

"Incredible. Just incredible." Samantha was hiding her smile behind a handful of popcorn.

"And his favorite television show is . . . the news." She was nodding seriously. "I think it's to his credit that he's so interested in world events."

I was dropping ice cubes into three tall glasses. "He sounds like a true intellectual."

"Oh, wow! You'll *never* guess what he eats for breakfast!"

"Orange juice?" I asked.

"Popcorn?" said Samantha.

"Cereal!" Carla announced triumphantly. "He eats cereal for breakfast, just like me!"

"Mind-boggling," said Samantha.

"Totally awesome," I added earnestly.

Carla looked up from the magazine. "You mean you don't find this the most fascinating thing in the entire world?"

I shrugged. "Sorry, Carla. I'm afraid I just can't get as worked up about this Johnny Rainbow as you."

"You'd feel differently if you ever heard him sing. And I promise you that once you see one of his videos, you'll never be the same."

"That sounds like a threat," Samantha observed.

"Well, I plan to check this Johnny Rainbow guy

out," I said sincerely. "If Carla's so crazy about him, he must be something special."

"I'm hardly the only one who's crazy about him," said Carla. "Two-thirds of all the females in America are madly in love with Johnny Rainbow. Maybe even two-thirds of all the females in the *world*!"

"Johnny Rainbow, huh?" I repeated, handing Carla a glass of orange juice. "I guess that's a name I should keep in mind."

The next morning, from the moment I woke up, there was only one thing I could think about: the fact that that evening was the opening of Carla's play. She had called late the night before, excited over how well the dress rehearsal had gone. It was all I could do to keep myself from telling her, "See? I told you so!" I had the feeling that Samantha had the same problem, too.

"Oooh, how am I ever going to sit through a whole day of classes?" Carla had moaned.

I was wondering the exact same thing as I tromped up the steps of good old Hanover Junior High School at twenty minutes before nine on Friday morning. It was going to be so much fun, seeing the play, watching Carla perform, and then afterward going to YoYo's Yogurt with her and Samantha to celebrate. Somehow, getting through a math quiz, a gym class, and a bunch of lectures was going to be tough.

I was thinking about the play—and how much more interesting my life had become since I moved to Hanover and became friends with Sam and Carla—as I walked into the school building. I was feeling pretty good, in fact. That is, until I noticed Wendy Lipton and Kicky Blake, dressed in their silly white sweaters, standing by the water fountain. That particular water fountain happens to be one of the school's most popular hangouts. It also happens to be close to my locker—only three lockers away from good old number 1207.

I wasn't exactly in the mood for those two. But what could I do? I had to hang up my jacket, and I had to get out the books I would be needing for the first three periods of the day.

Maybe, just maybe, I thought hopefully, Wendy and Kicky will ignore me.

No such luck.

"Well, if it isn't Little Miss Bubble Gum herself," said Kicky.

"Hi, Wendy. Hi, Kicky." I made a beeline for my locker, meanwhile keeping my head down.

"Made any new gum wrapper chains lately?" Wendy asked in this really phony, sickly sweet voice.

"Maybe you could sell them," Kicky suggested, smirking. "Maybe I'd even buy one."

"Me too," said Wendy. "Of course, I'd want to see a sample before I put in my order."

"Yeah, let's see your famous bubble gum wrapper chain," Kicky demanded.

"Why don't you just leave me alone?" My head was buried inside my locker as I tried to remember whether or not I needed to bring my grammar book to English class.

"So where is it, Betsy? I want to see if it's as great as you think it is."

All of a sudden, Wendy lunged toward me, grabbing my green canvas book bag out of my arms. Before I knew what was happening, she had it.

"Hey, give me that!" I cried, reaching for it.

But she was too fast for me. She had already torn the bag open and was sticking her hand inside.

"I bet you keep it in here," she said. "Where else would you keep something as *important* as a bubble gum chain?"

"Wendy, this isn't funny!" I cried.

I reached for the bag again. But just as I got close, she pulled it away. And then she pulled out the paper chain, a look of evil triumph on her face.

"So *this* is it?" she yelped. "All that fuss about this ugly thing?"

I just sighed, meanwhile folding my arms across my chest. "Wendy, I'm going to ask you one more time. Please give me my bag back. If you don't, I'm just going to go to Ms. Trayton's office—"

"Gonna get the school principal to fight your battles for you?" Kicky wheedled.

"Or maybe you should just get the other members of the Bubble Gum Gang to help you," Wendy taunted. "The three Miss Goody-Goodies, banded together."

And then the warning bell sounded. Wendy looked

startled for a moment. Then she tossed the book bag and the chain in my direction.

"Oh, take your stuff. Who wants it? Come on, Kicky. We'd better get to class, or we'll be late. I don't want to get detention again."

I was so mad that I could have screamed. But at the moment, it seemed much more important to get myself together and hurry off to my English class. Which is precisely what I did.

As I slid into my seat, the final bell was ringing. I was totally out of breath from running to class. Even so, I could hardly wait to tell Sam and Carla all about the little scene that had just transpired, and so I was hoping this would turn out to be one of those days when Mr. Homer started class a little bit late.

Let me explain something about my English teacher. Mr. Homer is a nice, gentle, capable man. He really is. But there's this other side to him, a side that comes across as—shall we say—somewhat flakey. He's always doing odd things, like forgetting to start class because he's so busy talking about football with Jason Downing and some of the other football "stars" in our class. One time he dropped an entire box of paper clips all over the floor. Millions of them, everywhere. Overall, he's the kind of teacher whom most kids like. But that doesn't stop some of the other kids from making jokes about him.

Still, the one thing that Mr. Homer had never done was *miss* a class. Or even be late, for that matter. Yet once I got my bearings and was beginning to start breathing like a normal person, I discovered that he was nowhere to be seen.

I decided to take advantage of our teacher's absence to fill Carla and Sam in.

"You two are never going to believe what just happened to me," I began. And then I told them.

"Poor Betsy!" Samantha exclaimed when I had finished.

"Those two are incredible!" Carla cried. "I think we should tell the principal what they did. They shouldn't be allowed to get away with it!"

"*I* think we should simply ignore them," Samantha said calmly. "You know that old saying, don't you? 'Just ignore them—maybe they'll go away'?"

"Sam's right," I said, sighing. "Sooner or later, they'll get tired of trying to make our lives miserable. Besides, they haven't done any real harm. They're just acting childish, that's all."

By that point, we were already more than five minutes into first period. And still there was no English teacher in sight.

"Where's Mr. Homer?" I asked, puzzled.

Samantha shrugged. "I don't know. He's never been late before, has he?"

"Maybe he's out sick," Carla suggested.

"If he were out sick, there would be a substitute in here already," I reminded them. "It's past five after. This is very strange, don't you think?"

I glanced around the classroom. All the other kids

were taking advantage of the teacher not being there, chattering away and having the time of their lives. Skip Jones and Ray Hutchinson, for example, were playing catch with some girl's pocketbook, ignoring her pleas that they stop. Nobody else besides us three looked particularly concerned.

But then again, nobody else besides us three was a member of the Bubble Gum Gang.

"What we just might have here," I said slowly, "is a new mystery for the Bubble Gum Gang to investigate."

"The Case of the Disappearing English Teacher?" Carla suggested.

"How about, 'Mr. Homer, Come Home'?" Samantha tried. She gave a little smile, as if she were proud of how clever she was being.

I was just about to offer my own idea when I noticed a dark figure looming in the doorway. I thought it might be suspect number one. But as I looked over, suddenly hopeful, I saw that it was only Mr. Homer.

"So much for the Case of the Disappearing English Teacher," Carla said with a disappointed sigh.

I turned around in my seat so that I faced the front. I was expecting some dull explanation from Mr. Homer, something about how he was late because he had had an early morning dentist appointment. Or at least something humorous, like he was late because his dog ate his class notes for the day.

But the look on his face told me right away that

what he was about to tell us was anything but humorous.

"I'd like to explain to all of you why I was late this morning," he said in this very soft, very serious voice. "I'm afraid something terrible has happened."

I glanced over at Samantha, sitting beside me. But her eyes were glued to Mr. Homer's face.

"This morning," he went on in that same eerie tone, "when I left my house to come to school, I found that someone had vandalized my car."

"Vandalized your car!" I gasped. "What happened?"

Mr. Homer looked over in my direction as he continued to address the whole class. "Someone sprayed shaving cream all over it and let the air out of the tires."

A murmur rose up from the classroom.

"Boy, that's terrible," said one of the boys on the other side of the room.

"This is giving me the creeps," said one of the girls.

"At least it was nothing serious," Mr. Homer went on. "I've already hosed it down and arranged to get some more air in the tires. Still, I filed a report with the police this morning. They're looking into it."

"Do the police have any idea who might be responsible?" asked Samantha.

"Not yet," Mr. Homer said earnestly. "But they do have one clue that is helping to point them in the right direction."

"What's that?" a handful of kids asked.

As he looked out over the classroom, the expression on his face was strained.

"From the size of the footprints that were found in the mud near my driveway, it looks as if the vandals could well have been somebody from this school."

chapter
four

"Vandals—right here in Hanover!" exclaimed Carla as we sat around the kitchen table at her house right after school that Friday. "It's hard to believe. And as if *that* weren't bad enough in itself, why on earth would anybody pick on poor Mr. Homer?"

I simply shrugged. I, for one, didn't have a clue.

Samantha didn't seem to, either. In fact, she was surprisingly quiet.

"Sam?" I asked. "What do *you* think of all this?"

"I don't know what to think," she replied. "But I've been wondering if it might be time for the Bubble Gum Gang to do a little investigating."

Shaking my head, I said, "I thought of that, too. But Mr. Homer said the police were investigating this. I think that pretty much puts it out of our league."

"I suppose you're right." Samantha sighed. "I just wish there were something we could do."

"Well, I'm just as upset about this as anybody," Carla said, standing up. "And I hope they catch the troublemakers, whoever they are. But right now, I've got a few jillion things to do. Wash my hair, iron my costume, go over my lines, try to remember that being in a school play is not a matter of life and death. . . ."

"Poor Carla!" Samantha cried. "Are you getting nervous?"

She made a funny face. "I'll be fine, once I get out there on stage. I *know* that. It's just that *thinking* about doing certain things is sometimes harder than just *doing* them."

I gave a sympathetic laugh. "Don't worry, Carla. You're going to be fantastic. And don't forget that Sam and I will be sitting in the front row with your family, rooting for you."

"Just think," Sam told her, sounding wistful. "You're going out there as a member of the Bubble Gum Gang, but you're coming back a star!"

"And in case you do get a *little* bit nervous before going on stage," I said, "I have just the thing to keep your mouth from getting dry."

I handed her a piece of bubble gum.

"Is it just me," I wondered aloud, "or are there butterflies in your stomach, too?"

"I've got dozens," Samantha replied. "Maybe even hundreds."

It was five minutes to eight, and just as we had promised, Samantha and I were sitting in the front row of our school auditorium. On our right were Carla's mother, her father, and her older sister, Kelly. On our left were a few aunts and uncles and cousins, various people whose names I never did manage to get straight.

The place was packed. The Drama Club's publicity committee had done an incredible job of putting the word out. Posters were hung on every bulletin board in school, daily announcements were made over the loudspeaker during homeroom, and letters were sent home to all the parents. A full-page ad had recently run in the local paper, too.

Their efforts had paid off so well, in fact, that Sam and I and Carla's relatives were lucky to get such good seats. Of course, not everybody in the audience was interested in sitting a mere ten feet from the stage.

"It's great, sitting so close," Samantha observed. "We'll be able to hear everything, to see everything. . . . We won't miss a single detail. It's almost like being in the play ourselves!"

"So *that* explains the butterflies!" I replied, giggling. "*We* know that we're just part of the audience, but nobody has bothered to mention that to our stomachs!"

As soon as the play started, the butterflies joined everybody else in the auditorium in becoming part of a silent, enraptured audience. And just as we had been hoping, the whole thing went without a single hitch.

We were all transported to another time and another place. We met characters we had never met before—and we began to believe they were real. Everyone did well. Even Wendy did an acceptable job.

But the cast's brightest light was, without a doubt, our pal Carla. She was mesmerizing, to put it mildly. What a performance! While the other kids in the play were doing a more-or-less competent job of acting, I got the feeling that Carla really believed she was her character. When the play ended and the audience burst into wild applause, there were tears in my eyes.

"You were right. A star is born," I commented to Samantha as we pulled on our coats and joined the crowds shuffling out of the auditorium.

"She was good, wasn't she?" Samantha was beaming proudly. "Carla really can act!"

Not surprisingly, Carla was all smiles and giggles as we met her backstage. She was surrounded not only by her family but also by the rest of the cast, who were all offering one another congratulations. But as I stood on the sidelines, watching, I could see that somehow, every time people congratulated Carla, there was a kind of sincerity—awe, almost—in their voices.

The Drama Club's adviser, Ms. Hart, was grinning from ear to ear. She was carrying around the bouquet of red roses that the cast had bought for her, presenting them to her onstage at the end of the performance. It was clear she couldn't be happier with the way things had gone.

"The play was great," I told her after pushing my way through the excited crowd. "Everybody did a wonderful job. And Carla was terrific."

Ms. Hart looked at me and smiled. "Carla always does a terrific job."

"I'm totally bowled over," I told Carla for the five hundredth time as, half an hour later, she sat across from me and Samantha at a small table in the window of YoYo's Yogurt. "I never dreamed you could act that well!"

Carla was smiling so broadly that it was difficult for her to spoon her chocolate yogurt sundae inside her mouth. It was just as well, since after the three of us held our own private little celebration, she was heading over to one of the other Drama Club member's houses for the cast party. Rumor had it that there was going to be a huge cake on hand, with "Congratulations to the Cast and Crew of *Our Town*!" written across the top in frosting. And as if *that* weren't enough celebrating, the following morning her whole family, including all those aunts and uncles and cousins, were going out for brunch—in her honor, of course.

"It was so much fun," she said, her eyes shining. "It's hard to explain, but there's something magical about being on stage in front of an audience."

"Especially since you seem to have become the character you were playing," Samantha observed. "That really is a kind of magic."

"I wish you two could experience it, too," Carla went on dreamily.

"Not me!" I croaked. "I can barely manage to give an oral book report in English class, much less be in a play!"

Samantha laughed. "I think I'd get terrible stage fright, too. In fact, Carla, I can't imagine how on earth you do it."

"Well, it is a little bit hard," our star admitted. "Especially right before. I always hear these little voices in my head, saying, 'Are you *sure* you can do this? Are you sure you *want* to do this?' "

"I know all about those voices," Samantha said, chuckling. "But somehow, there's always a slightly louder voice, as well, saying, 'Oh, sure you can. And you will!' "

"Well, who knows?" Carla said. "Maybe one day you two will be in a play, too. Then you'll find out how much fun it is. And you'll see for yourselves what an incredible experience it is to be onstage."

"That's it!" I suddenly cried, dropping my spoon into my strawberry-banana surprise, one of YoYo's specialties. "I've got it! Inspiration has finally hit!"

I looked around the table and saw that both Samantha and Carla were looking at me as if I had suddenly started talking in Lithuanian.

"*What's* it?" Samantha asked gently. "Betsy, what on earth are you talking about?"

"Raising money to build a new school playground, that's what!"

Carla and Samantha exchanged puzzled looks.

"Were we just talking about raising money for a playground?" Samantha asked.

Carla shrugged. "Gee, and here I thought we were talking about putting on plays."

"We *are* talking about putting on plays," I said, so excited that I could hardly get the words out. Having a mouth full of strawberries and banana slices didn't help much, either. "*And* we're talking about raising money for the playground!"

Another puzzled look passed between my two buddies.

"Look," I said, exasperated not by their inability to understand as much as by my own inability to communicate. "It's simple. The way we raise money for the playground is by putting on a play!"

"A fund-raising event," Samantha said, her eyes suddenly glowing. "My mother and father go to those all the time. It's a great way to raise money for charity."

"I love your idea!" Carla exclaimed. "We could open it up to all the kids at school. Even kids who couldn't make the time for the Drama Club could be involved, since this would be a one-time event."

I really appreciated the fact that they were both jumping on the bandwagon, getting so excited so quickly.

"Maybe we should put it on in the elementary school auditorium," Samantha remarked, "since that's the school we're trying to raise money for."

Carla was shaking her head. "The high school auditorium is the biggest one in town. The more seats that are available, the more money we can raise . . . and the more quickly the new playground can get built!" She sighed. "Now all we have to do is pick a play. It should be one that has lots of people in the cast. That way, anyone who wants to be in it can."

"How about a musical?" Samantha suggested. "I can see it now: dozens of cast members, singing, dancing, wearing wonderful costumes. . . ."

"Maybe it shouldn't be too demanding," I pointed out. "I mean, we are dealing with amateurs here. Besides, with a musical, we'd need a full orchestra, a conductor, a really top-notch director. . . ."

Carla frowned. "This might be harder than we first thought. It's a great idea, Betsy, but how are we ever going to come up with a play that's just right?"

Slowly, a smile was creeping over my face. My brain was clicking away, churning out idea after idea, one vision after another of how we could approach this.

"Uh oh," Samantha said with a laugh. "I think Betsy is about to hatch another idea."

"I certainly hope so," Carla said. "We sure could use one!"

I looked at Carla, then at Samantha, then back at Carla. With a little shrug, I said, "A talent show."

Samantha's eyes grew big. "Of course! The perfect solution! We could open auditions to anybody who wants to be in it—"

"Even if they have no experience," Carla said.

"No matter what their talent happens to be!"

I nodded, wondering if I could reach back far enough to give myself a good, solid pat on the back. "The possibilities are endless!"

"It's a wonderful idea," Samantha cried. "People can sing or dance or play musical instruments or . . . or do birdcalls or play the spoons. . . ."

"And no matter what they do, all their friends will come to watch them." Carla looked ready to burst. "And that means we'll raise lots and lots of money for the playground!"

I frowned. "How much do you think we should charge for tickets?"

"Four dollars, at least," said Samantha.

But Carla was shaking her head. "Five dollars, easily."

I laughed. "That turned out to be an easy decision to make. Speaking of decisions, we'll need to choose just the right person to be our Mistress of Ceremonies. It's an important job, probably the most important in the entire production. We'll need someone who's comfortable up onstage. Someone who can do a good job of introducing each act. And, of course, someone who'll have no problem keeping the audience entertained."

"If you're looking for a volunteer," Carla said shyly, her cheeks turning pink, "I guess I . . . maybe . . . if you think it's all right. . . ."

"Carla," I said, grinning, "the part is yours."

I reached for my spoon and dug into my strawberry-banana surprise. The only trouble was that now *I* was grinning so broadly that I could barely eat.

chapter
five

Over the next few days, I ate, drank, slept, and breathed talent show. Now that I'd gotten my inspiration, nothing was going to stop me from making it happen.

During the weekend, Carla was busy with the play, of course, since the Drama Club put it on again on Saturday night and then once more on Sunday afternoon. But once she was finished making theater history, she joined Samantha and me in our crazed efforts to get our fund-raiser off the ground.

The first thing we did was check with Ms. Franklin, the principal of the Hanover Elementary School. Is it any surprise that she thought it was a fine idea? In fact, she seemed overwhelmed by our interest in helping the school build a new playground. And she offered to help in any way she could.

Next, we had to pick a time and a place to hold the show. We planned it for the Saturday night that was two weekends away, far away enough from the run of

Our Town to keep people from feeling overwhelmed, but long enough before Thanksgiving that our potential ticket buyers wouldn't yet be busy with turkeys and pumpkin pies. We also got permission to hold all the rehearsals, as well as the big night itself, in the high school auditorium.

Those were the first steps. After that, the project seemed to take on a life of its own. I put Samantha in charge of posters. She didn't waste any time before recruiting kids in the Art Club who were dying for a chance to show off their talent. Carla, meanwhile, was given the job of telephoning the local newspapers, getting the word out about the student talent show. And I got busy setting up the auditions.

I approached Ms. Hart first, since I knew she had experience with this kind of thing.

"What you need to look for," she told me, "is the person who can do something—anything—very, very well. And if he or she is a little bit of a ham, that doesn't hurt either!"

In addition to giving me that good, solid piece of advice, she told me I was welcome to use her classroom for the auditions. I set them up for Tuesday, at seven o'clock in the evening. That way, even kids who were busy with after-school clubs and sports could make it to the tryouts.

"How are we ever going to choose?" I wailed at five minutes before seven. Everything was ready. Sam, Carla, and I were sitting behind the big desk in the front of the classroom, trying to look like we knew what we were doing. Each one of us had a pad of paper and a pen, so we could make notes. I also had a clipboard so the auditioners could sign in. We had even cleared away the desks to make a little "stage."

"Just remember what Ms. Hart said," Carla insisted. She peeked out the door. "Uh, did she happen to mention how we should handle a crowd that could barely fit inside the Superbowl?"

I just stared at her. "You're kidding . . . right?"

Samantha stuck her head out the door. "She's not kidding."

"Well," I told them, smiling weakly, "I suppose that having too many people show up is better than not having enough!"

I could scarcely believe how many of the students at our school thought they had enough talent to get up on a stage and perform. I panicked as I went into the hall to call the first person in line. There were more people out there than I ever would have dreamed—forty, at least. Some were wearing costumes. One girl, who I recognized as a seventh grader, was wearing silver tap shoes with a short, sequined skirt and a feathered hat. Three eighth-grade girls were dressed up like teddy bears, each with a different color ribbon tied around her neck. There was a ninth-grade boy dressed in an Uncle Sam costume; I could hardly wait to see what his talent was.

Some people were carrying musical instruments. A clarinet, a guitar . . . would you believe that somebody actually brought a tuba? A few would-be singers were practicing scales, and an aspiring magician kept pulling a quarter out from behind the ear of the boy right in front of him—much to the other boy's annoyance.

Still, what struck me most was how hopeful they all looked. It was clear that each one was excited over the prospect of being in a talent show. I knew I had seen the look in their eyes before. It was the same one I saw on Carla's face every time she talked about acting.

"Okay, who's first?" I called. "Come on in and sign your name on this clipboard. Write your telephone number, your talent, and exactly what you would like to do in the show."

Over the next two hours, Carla, Samantha, and I were treated to the most bizarre string of acts imaginable. There were a lot of singers, dancers, musicians, and comedians; that much, I had expected. What I didn't expect was a boy who I knew was active in the Chess Club, playing his nose. That's right, his nose. He kind of twanged it, as if it were some kind of musical instrument—one that just happened to be attached to his body.

I didn't expect a ninth-grade girl who did imitations of worms. She was quite interesting, actually, slithering across the floor and doing other wormlike things. It was certainly something I had never seen before. I had also never seen anyone do a gymnastics routine on one of those small trampolines, recite a poem that contained puns based on the names of every country on the continent of Africa, or juggle six cordless phones without dropping a single one, or even accidentally dialing.

The way we had decided to go about choosing the best of the would-be stars was for me, Sam, and Carla to rate each performer on a one-to-ten scale—ten being ready for prime-time television and one being a complete embarrassment to every living, breathing creature on this planet. I had thought it would be easy, but boy, was I wrong. I mean, how do you rate somebody who acts so much like a real worm that you keep waiting for some giant bird to swoop down and gobble her up? From the faces my two buddies kept making, I could tell they were having the same difficulty.

Finally, when I thought I could stand no more, I stepped out into the hall one more time and discovered there was nobody else waiting.

"Yea!" I cheered. "That's it!"

"You mean we're done?" Dramatically Carla clutched both hands to her heart. "I thought they'd never leave!"

As usual, Samantha was much more philosophical. "What a fascinating bunch. I had no idea there was so much talent in our school! Should we start comparing scores now, or do you think we should wait until we've had a chance to think?"

"Excuse me, are we too late?" a squeaky voice called in from the hallway. "Are the auditions over?"

"Can we manage one more?" I asked, concerned

more about my own ability to sit through still another act than that of my two friends.

I was expecting another singer or dancer, or maybe a Swiss yodeler dressed in leather shorts. I did *not* expect Wendy Lipton and Kicky Blake—precisely who happened to be standing in the doorway of Ms. Hart's classroom.

"It's *you*?" Kicky cried. "*You're* the ones who are running the auditions?"

"That's right," Carla replied, her chin suddenly stuck high in the air. "We're the ones who came up with the idea of raising money to build the new playground; we're the ones who thought up the talent show; and we're the ones who are putting the whole thing together."

"Great," Wendy mumbled. "Now that we know, do you think we're wasting our time, Kicky?"

"You're welcome to audition," Samantha said politely. I must say, her sense of diplomacy never fails to amaze me.

Kicky shrugged. "We might as well. I mean, we're here, aren't we?"

"Uh, what exactly is your talent?" I asked, my pen poised above my notepad.

"We sing," Wendy replied. With a giggle, she added, "We're kind of like a sister act."

So that explains why they're still dressing the same, I thought, wearing those ridiculous fuzzy white sweaters with the tigers on one side.

"Did you bring music?" Samantha asked. She had

already settled into a chair, and she was actually managing to look interested.

"Music?" Wendy repeated. "Uh, what do you mean?"

"Something to sing along with," Carla explained, not even trying to sound patient. "You know, instruments? Songs? Something that will be going on in the background while you're going on in the foreground?"

"Oh. You mean like an instrumental tape or something," said Kicky.

"*Now* you've got it."

"No, we just . . . sing."

"Okay, then," I said. "Whenever you're ready."

The two sweater girls stood in front of the three of us, their faces bright and eager. After Kicky muttered, "Ah-one, ah-two, ah-one, two, three, four," they began to sing.

How can I possibly explain the way they sounded? What words could possibly convey the sounds that came out of their mouths? Fire alarms? Fingernails screeching against a blackboard? Maybe I'm being too kind.

"So?" Wendy said after the two of them had muddled their way through what seemed to be a song from the radio. "What do you think?"

"You know, Wendy," Carla said. "if you kept those angora sweaters of yours in the freezer, they wouldn't get little white fuzzies all over everything."

"Huh?" Wendy and Kicky just looked at each other.

"Uh, I think what Carla means," Samantha said quickly, "is that we can't really discuss our reaction until all three of us have had a chance to sit down and compare our notes."

Wendy shrugged. "We know we're good. It's just a question of how strong the competition is."

"What song was that, exactly, that you were singing?" Samantha asked pleasantly, getting ready to write.

"Why, that's Johnny Rainbow's latest hit," Kicky answered, looking at Sam as if there were potatoes growing out of her ears. "You mean you've never heard it?"

"I love that song," Carla said. To herself, she muttered, "At least, I did until tonight."

"I just *adore* Johnny Rainbow," Wendy was gushing. "Don't you? I buy every one of his albums the second it hits the stores. And I buy every magazine that prints even a single word about him. Did you see the latest issue of *Rockers 'n' Rollers* magazine? It had all kinds of cool secrets about him. They even told what he eats for *breakfast*!"

"Cereal," I replied matter-of-factly. It's amazing how much information the human mind can absorb. "Okay, Wendy, Kicky. Thanks a lot for auditioning. We'll be notifying people really soon, since the talent show is being held in less than two weeks."

"Gee, less than two weeks. Do you think we have

enough time to get our costumes ready?'' Kicky was asking Wendy as the two of them wandered out the door.

The moment they were gone, Carla and Sam and I looked at one another—and then burst out laughing.

''Come on, you two,'' I said, gathering up my things. ''Let's get out of here.''

I grabbed my green book bag and pushed the clipboard and my notepad inside. I also had to scrounge around, looking for my change purse so I could find a quarter to call my mother and tell her it was time for her to pick us up. As I did, I got the feeling there was something wrong. I couldn't quite figure it out . . . and before I had a chance to put two and two together, another strange voice called in to us from the corridor.

''Excuse me, but are you finished in there yet?''

''Oh, *no*!'' I moaned. ''Not *another* one!''

I looked at Carla and Sam. They looked just as horrified as I was.

But then the stranger peeked through the door. He was wearing a costume, all right. And with his bucket and mop, he made a very convincing custodian.

''If you girls are through, I'll get started cleaning this classroom up.''

The poor man never did understand why the three of us started laughing so hard.

The next morning, I was still flying high, as thrilled as could be that the talent show was really starting to come together. Carla and Sam and I had yet to sit down and compare our notes, but I was already getting a pretty clear idea of who was going to make it into our talent show—and who was going to have to seek fame and fortune somewhere else.

As I sat in homeroom, waiting impatiently for English class so I could tell Sam and Carla some of the earth-shattering ideas I had had in the last twelve hours, I was doodling away fiendishly. But instead of just drawing weird designs that look like the kind of view you get from looking through a kaleidoscope, the way I usually do, I was designing the cover of the program. I was even excited about *that*. A few curlicues here, a couple of stars over there. . . .

Just as I was trying to decide whether to have the programs printed on blue paper or something a bit more eye-catching, like maybe neon pink or orange, my homeroom teacher, Mr. Arden, came rushing into the room.

"May I have everyone's attention, please?" he demanded.

He looked pretty upset. That immediately got me interested, since Mr. Arden is a math teacher. The only time I've ever seen him get upset about *anything* was the time he overheard somebody saying that computers were one of the worst things that had ever happened to civilization as we know it. Other than that, he's always been Mr. Calm, approaching everything totally logically, without a drop of emotion.

Not this time. I put down my pen, forgetting all about the pale blue versus neon pink debate.

"I have some bad news to report," Mr. Arden said. "I'm sure that most of you have heard about the act of vandalism that occurred a few days ago."

"Right," somebody called out from the back of the classroom. "Somebody vandalized the car that belongs to that English teacher, Mr. Homer, right?"

"Exactly." Mr. Arden frowned. "Well, as if that weren't bad enough, I just found out that a second act of vandalism has been committed."

Vandalism here in Hanover . . . *again*? My eyes nearly fell out of my head.

"What happened?" someone else asked.

"Last night, somebody sprayed shaving cream all over one of the classrooms. It wasn't discovered until this morning, when the teacher whose room it is walked in."

"Was any serious damage done?" I asked.

"Fortunately not. It was mostly the desks and chairs that were sprayed. They're easy enough to clean off. But some of the shaving cream got on the bulletin boards. A few of the posters, as well as some student projects that were on display, were totally ruined."

"At least nothing major was destroyed," I observed, trying to be optimistic. Not that I was doing a very good job. My heart felt as if someone had snuck over and plunked a big, heavy paperweight on it.

"Which classroom was it?" asked a boy sitting in

back. Chuckling, he added, ''Maybe the biology test I was supposed to have today will be canceled.''

"No such luck,'' Mr. Arden replied. ''The classroom that was vandalized was Ms. Hart's room.''

chapter
six

"Did you hear?" I cried the moment I reached Mr. Homer's classroom.

As usual, Samantha and Carla were already in their seats. What was not usual, however, were the looks on their faces. They both looked as if they had just seen a ghost . . . or maybe even something worse.

"I can't believe it," Samantha said, her voice nearly a whisper. "The same thing happening all over again. . . ."

"And in Ms. Hart's classroom!" Carla interrupted. And then, after swallowing hard, she came out with exactly what we were all thinking but were afraid to say. "Do you think anyone will assume that we . . . ?"

"Okay, everybody." Mr. Homer clapped his hands just then, cutting her off. It was just as well, as far as I was concerned. This was something I was in no hurry to deal with.

"We have a lot of ground to cover," he went on

cheerfully, as if nothing out of the ordinary were happening. Which, for ninety percent of the people in the room, it wasn't. It was that other ten percent—we three members of the Bubble Gum Gang—that was going to have real trouble concentrating on today's lecture on commonly misspelled words.

"All right, let's take it from the top." Mr. Homer turned toward the blackboard, a piece of chalk in his hand. I could tell he was really excited about this. I only wished I could share some of his enthusiasm. "Who knows how to spell 'accommodate?' "

I knew exactly how to spell "accommodate." But my heart wasn't in improving my mind. I was too busy agonizing over this second act of vandalism—and where it might lead.

It didn't take me long to find out. Mr. Homer had just started on commonly misspelled words beginning with the letter *B* when Ms. Marks, one of the secretaries who works in the main office, popped her head in the doorway.

"Excuse me, Mr. Homer," she said in a very earnest tone of voice. "May I speak with you in the hall for a moment?"

Mr. Homer looked a little miffed over being interrupted just as he was about to spell "benign" for the class. But he went out into the hallway. I could hear him and Ms. Marks talking quietly. I was tempted to look over at Sam and Carla, but I didn't dare. Instead, I just stared at my notebook, where I had just written the word "benign" in neat, careful letters.

When Mr. Homer returned to the classroom, instead of heading back toward the blackboard, he came over to where I was sitting. Matter-of-factly, but in a soft voice, he said, "Betsy, Samantha, Carla, Ms. Trayton wants to see the three of you."

Ms. Trayton, the school principal. As if I were in the least bit surprised.

I felt like a robot as I stood up, moving without really thinking about it, going through the motions without actually *feeling* anything. Except dread, that is. But that was buried somewhere deep inside, not too far from the pit of my stomach.

It wasn't until I was in the corridor with my two friends that I dared to look at them.

"Look," Carla said quickly, "all we have to do is explain that it wasn't us."

"But we were the ones who had the use of that room last night!" I said, trying not to sound as upset as I was feeling.

"But we're innocent!" Samantha exclaimed. "You know it, I know it, Carla knows it."

"Yes, of course we're innocent." I let out a deep sigh. "The problem is, now it's up to us to convince Ms. Trayton of that."

As the three of us sat in the waiting area of the school's main office, watching Ms. Marks and the other two secretaries busily typing and filing and talking on the telephone as if everything were perfectly normal, I was reminded of the last time we had found ourselves in that position. It had been less than a week since the Bubble Gum Gang had gone into the principal's office at the elementary school, anxious to find out what was going on with the playground.

And now here we were again. Sitting in a waiting room in a school's main office, waiting to talk to the principal. Only it was a different school. And a different principal. And the reason why we were there was very, very different.

"All we need to do," Samantha was saying, "is tell our side of it." She was trying to sound as if she were in control. But I could hear the way her voice was shaking, just the teensiest bit. "I'm sure Ms. Trayton will believe us."

"She'd better," Carla mumbled. "Because if she doesn't, we're all in big trouble."

And then the moment of truth arrived. Ms. Trayton appeared in the doorway of her office. I searched her face, looking for a trace of a smile. There was none.

"Come in, girls," she said, motioning for us to follow her. Then, once we were inside her office, she invited us, in a very formal, no-nonsense voice, to sit down.

I had never before in my life been called into the principal's office. In fact, I was always one of those students that the principal held up to everybody else as an example. Not that being in that position didn't cause problems of its own, at least where fitting in with the other kids was concerned. But at least I had never had to worry about being in the hot seat.

But there I was. In the hot seat. Not only me, either; my two best friends, as well.

"I'll get right to the point," Ms. Trayton said, still standing up but leaning against the edge of her desk. "First, let me ask you if you've heard about this second act of vandalism. The one that was just discovered this morning."

All three of us nodded.

"Then you know that the classroom in which the shaving cream was sprayed was Ms. Hart's room."

More nodding.

"The same room the three of you were given special permission to use last night."

So far, not one of us had said a single word.

Ms. Trayton drew her lips together in a thin, straight line. "All right, then. I'm going to come straight out and ask you. Were any of you three girls responsible for the mess that was made in there?"

"No!" This time, we all had something to say, and we all said it at exactly the same time. It would have been funny if this whole thing weren't so terrible.

Ms. Trayton nodded. "That's pretty much the response I was expecting."

Carla leaned forward in her seat. "Ms. Trayton, if we can just explain—"

But Ms. Trayton held up her hand to stop her from going on.

"I asked Ms. Marks to get your school records out before I called you in this morning," she said. She walked around to the other side of her desk. On it were three manila folders. "All three of you have impeccable school records. Not one single incident of any sort has ever been reported, going all the way back to kindergarten.

"And you're all good students. You, especially, Betsy. Why, I don't believe you've ever gotten anything less than an *A*."

"I got a *B*-plus in gym once," I muttered.

"So it's difficult to believe that any of you could have been involved in something like this. Yet you must admit that, since it was the three of you, and only you, who had access to that classroom, that you girls were the last ones to use it last night—"

All of a sudden, I jumped up. "The custodian!" I cried, snapping my fingers.

Needless to say, Ms. Trayton looked startled. "Excuse me, Betsy?"

"The custodian!" I repeated.

She, of course, had no idea what I was talking about. But Sam and Carla did. Their faces lit up like sparklers on the Fourth of July.

"Of course, the custodian!" Samantha exclaimed. "Why didn't we remember him sooner?"

"We're saved," Carla breathed.

Ms. Trayton shook her head in confusion. "Please, will somebody explain what you're talking about?"

Since Samantha and Carla looked over at me, I tackled that job myself.

"Ms. Trayton, the three of us left Ms. Hart's classroom last night at about ten minutes after nine. But we weren't the last ones in there. As we were leaving, the custodian came in to clean up.''

"That's right," Carla chimed in. "He's our witness. He saw for himself that when we finished with the auditions, the classroom was in tip-top shape."

"He saw us leave, too," Samantha remembered. "He was just coming in with his bucket and mop as we were putting on our jackets. . . ."

"And Betsy was looking through her book bag, trying to find a quarter so she could call her mother to ask her to come pick us up."

"What probably happened," said Sam, "is that after we left the school and after the custodian cleaned up in there, *then* the troublemakers went in to Ms. Hart's classroom and sprayed the shaving cream."

"We *are* innocent, Ms. Trayton," I said, my voice sounding just a little bit pleading. "And the custodian will back us up. All you have to do is ask him."

By now there was an odd look on the principal's face. I couldn't tell if she was impressed by our skill at solving mysteries—even mysteries that suddenly seemed to be involving us—or if she still didn't quite believe us.

At any rate, she wasted no time in picking up the telephone and asking Ms. Marks to get Mr. James, the night custodian, on the line. A few moments later, she was talking to him.

"Mr. James," she said calmly, "there are three girls here in my office who say you can verify the fact that last night, shortly after nine o'clock, they left

Ms. Hart's classroom to go home. They claim that the classroom was in perfect order, exactly the way they had found it.''

There was a long pause. And then, ''I see. I see. All right, then. Thank you, Mr. James. Good-bye.''

This time, the look on her face was one that I recognized. She looked apologetic. Maybe even a little bit sheepish. At that moment, that expression was more beautiful to me than the famous smile on the painting, the Mona Lisa.

''You were right,'' she said. ''Mr. James backed up your story one hundred percent. I'm sorry if I made you uncomfortable, but since you were the ones who used Ms. Hart's classroom last night, I'm sure you see why I had to speak with you about this incident.''

''I understand,'' I said, nodding.

''Ms. Trayton,'' Carla said, ''may we please be excused now?''

Never before in my life had I so looked forward to hearing a lecture on commonly misspelled words.

''What a relief!'' Carla collapsed against the row of metal lockers right outside the main office. ''Remind me to put being called into the principal's office on my list of the ten worst experiences in the world!''

''I think I'd better add it to my list, too,'' I said. ''I don't know about you two, but I'm still shaking.''

''Let's just hope that nothing like that ever happens again,'' said Samantha.

"Or if it does," Carla added, "that there's a custodian on the sidelines, ready to prove our innocence!"

Now that that ordeal was over, the three of us were in the best of moods. I was already starting to think about the talent show again. Where had I left off? Oh, yes, I remembered. Pale blue versus neon pink.

But Samantha had an even better plan in mind.

"Look, while we're walking back to English, why don't we put our heads together and decide who's going to be in our talent show?"

"Great idea," I said. "Then we can write up a list really fast and post it on the bulletin board outside the cafeteria."

Carla was grinning. "I'm glad I've already got a part. It's nice not to have to be sweating this one out."

"Not only do you have a part," I reminded her, "you've got the most important part in the entire production! Being Mistress of Ceremonies means you're going to run the whole thing."

Carla's dark eyes were twinkling. "I can hardly wait!"

It didn't take us long to pick the twelve best amateur entertainers out of the crowd that had auditioned the night before. I was afraid we would disagree on a few of them, but it was clear to all three of us who the performers with real talent were.

"So much for the human earthworm," I joked as

we headed back into our English class. "Maybe if she switched to reptiles . . . ?"

Coincidentally, Carla and I shared fifth-period lunch. By the time it rolled around, I had our list all drawn up. Sometimes it helps to have neat handwriting. She and I tacked it up on the bulletin board, patted each other on the back for the terrific job we were doing so far, and went into the cafeteria to hustle up some well-deserved grub.

It was while we were sitting together over tuna-fish sandwiches and cartons of low-fat chocolate milk that our *next* ordeal began.

"Oh, no," I muttered, being the first one to notice that there was some sort of commotion outside the cafeteria, right in front of the bulletin board. "What *now*?"

Carla craned her neck to see. "Uh-oh. Here comes the gruesome twosome. And they look *mad*."

Not that I was surprised. Even as I had been copying over the list of people who had made it into the talent show, I was dreading Kicky and Wendy's reaction. After all, their names hadn't made it onto the list.

And now, as the old saying goes, it was time to pay the piper.

"Where are they?" Wendy was fuming as she stomped into the cafeteria. She stood just inside, her hands on her hips, her eyes narrowed into mean little slits as she surveyed the crowded room.

"Abracadabra, hoozily-hoo," Carla muttered,

closing her eyes and scrunching her shoulders together. And then, snapping her eyes open again: "Betsy, did it work? Am I invisible?"

"Come on," I said. "Don't be afraid of those two."

"I suppose they couldn't do anything *really* terrible to us in front of all these people . . . could they?"

I sighed. "I'm sure they'll come up with something good."

"*There* they are!" Kicky suddenly shrieked.

To be honest, there was so much noise in the cafeteria that it's possible that not *everybody* in the place heard her. But I sure did. Without even meaning to, I found myself slumping down low in my chair.

But, like Carla, making myself invisible was one talent I did not possess. Kicky and Wendy stormed across the cafeteria and over to our table.

"Well?" Wendy demanded, folding her arms across her chest. "What do you two have to say for yourselves?"

"Nice sweaters," Carla said matter-of-factly. "Too bad I'm allergic to angora."

"Ha, ha. Very funny," Wendy countered. "That's so funny I forgot to laugh."

"Gee, I haven't heard that one in awhile," said Carla. "Not since I was six years old."

"You know what we're talking about," said Kicky. "The talent show."

"Oh, right," Carla said. "You know, I almost forgot all about that."

Wendy just glared at her. "We saw the list. So?"

"So?" I repeated.

"So why aren't our names on it?"

"Uh, Wendy," I stammered, "you know a lot of people tried out for the show last night. Dozens of people. And it wasn't an easy thing, trying to pick out—"

"Don't lie to me, Betsy." Wendy leaned over, looking at me with piercing eyes. "I know *exactly* why our names aren't on that list."

"Then why are you asking us?" Carla said under her breath.

"It's because you don't like us, that's why." Wendy tossed her head triumphantly. "It's clear that your choices were not based on talent. If they were, our names would be at the top of that list. You just wouldn't let us be in your stupid old show because you're *jealous*."

I kept my gaze fixed on the corner of the table. Out of the corner of my eye, I could see Carla shaking her head and rolling her eyes upward.

"Well, I have news for you two," Wendy went on, her voice sounding like a hiss. "And you can tell that snob, Samantha, too. This little talent show of yours is going to be a complete flop. Nobody's going to come, and you're not going to raise a penny. The three of you are going to end up the laughingstock of this town."

"Oh, really?" asked Carla politely. "May I ask

how you propose to accomplish all that—and still have time for cheerleading practice?''

"I don't know—yet," Wendy shot back. "But don't you worry. I'll think of something. And when I do, you'll know all about it. You, and everybody else around here."

"Oh, I'm scared," Carla said dryly. "I'm really scared." Turning to me, she said, "Betsy, do you by any chance have a tissue? I forgot to get a paper napkin, and my fingers are all sticky from the tuna fish."

"Sure," I replied, reaching for my book bag.

"Come on, Kicky," Wendy barked, turning on her heel. "I don't think I can take another *second* of these two."

"I thought they'd never leave," Carla said, sounding exasperated.

I laughed. "Do you really need a tissue, or were you just trying to get rid of them?"

She held up her hands for me to see. "Nope. I really, really need a tissue."

"Okay. Just give me a second." I started rummaging around in my book bag. A pen, a small pad of paper, my change purse. . . .

"Do you really think they're going to do something to get back at us?" I asked, still shuffling through all my junk.

"No way," Carla insisted. "Those two are all talk and no action. Besides, what could they possibly do to ruin a talent show as wonderful as the one we've got planned?"

At that point, I could hear her talking, but I was no longer listening. As I was scrounging around in my book bag, still trying to find a tissue for Carla, something had suddenly snapped into place. I realized what had struck me the evening before, the puzzled feeling I had gotten but never did take the time to figure out.

The bubble gum wrapper chain was gone.

chapter
seven

I decided not to mention the disappearance of the bubble gum chain to Carla or Samantha. At least, not yet—not until I had figured out what could have happened to it.

There are only two possibilities, I thought later that evening. I was taking a long walk after dinner, kicking through the dry leaves and trying to sort through the avalanche of events of the past few days. One is that I took it out and put it somewhere else. But I don't remember doing that . . . and I can't imagine why I would.

That pretty much let number one out, unless somewhere along the line I had developed a case of amnesia. Number two was a much stronger possibility.

It must have fallen out, I decided. I'm always putting things in and taking things out of that bag, and somewhere along the line, it must have just dropped out. I was probably in a hurry, and so I just didn't notice.

Having decided that that was the explanation for this "mystery," I made up my mind to check all the obvious places. The bottom of my locker, around the desk I have in my room . . . maybe even the school's lost and found. Sure, I was disappointed to have lost something that was so important to me. But if it didn't turn up, I could always make another one. That thought gave me enough comfort that I was finally able to go home and concentrate on getting my home-work done.

By the next morning, I had all but forgotten about the bubble gum wrapper chain. The minute I hit English class, Carla and Sam pounced on me, practically bursting with all the great ideas they had had about the talent show.

"Betsy," Samantha said excitedly, "I called the local newspaper and talked the advertising manager into giving us a big ad for half their usual rate, since it's a fund-raising event and all. The ad's coming out this weekend. I told them to print that the tickets are five dollars each. That is what we agreed, right?"

"Look, Betsy!" Carla cried. "I've started writing up jokes I can use to introduce the different acts in the show. Could you read them over and tell me what you think?"

"Oooh, I almost forgot to tell you. My father said he'd get the programs printed up for us, as his dona-tion," Samantha went on. "All he needs to know is exactly what we want them to say. Oh, and he also needs a decision about what color to make them."

"No question," I replied. "Neon pink. Carla, I think telling a few jokes between acts is a great idea. Here, let me see what you've got so far."

I was reading a really funny line about the food in the school cafeteria when I got the creepy feeling that somebody was watching me. I whirled around and discovered that Skip Jones was standing a few feet away, just staring.

"Hi, Skip," I said weakly.

"What?" he shot back. "You mean you actually *talk* to people who aren't in your special club? What's that stupid thing called? The Bubble Gum Girls?"

"The Bubble Gum Gang. And it's not stupid."

"Oh, yeah? Well, it just so happens that that's a matter of opinion."

Carla quickly came to my rescue.

"Come on, Betsy," she said, glaring at Skip. "You'd better hurry if you want to read that before class starts."

For the rest of the morning, I was so wrapped up in planning the talent show that I forgot all about nasty old Skip Jones. I also forgot about the missing bubble gum chain. Not surprisingly, I even forgot all about the threats Wendy and Kicky had made the day before.

Not for long. Right after the period bell had rung, Carla and I headed toward the school cafeteria, still talking about the talent show.

"Now here's an idea I want you to consider," Carla was saying. "How about me wearing a costume?

Maybe even a few costumes. Here's my idea: I thought I could wear something simple, like a plain, dark dress, and then in between each act come out wearing something different with it. A big hat with feathers one time, a Frankenstein mask another, a pair of red rubber boots another . . . what do you think?"

I laughed. "I think you were born to be in show biz, Carla. Even if it turns out that nobody likes the talent acts we've picked, everybody in the audience is going to adore *you*!"

Suddenly, I stopped. I froze, in fact. My eyes nearly popped out of my head.

There, taped to the wall right in front of the entrance to the cafeteria, was a huge poster, nearly four feet by four feet.

"Come to the Party of the Year!" was handwritten across the top with red marker. "THE WILDEST, CRAZIEST, BEST PARTY YOU'VE EVER BEEN TO IN YOUR LIFE!"

Then, right below, "Sponsored by The Cheerleaders of Hanover Junior High School."

And then, below *that*, "Live Rock Band! Free Snacks! Door Prizes . . . and Sur-prizes! Only three dollars a person!"

But the part that really hit me in the stomach was the date. The cheerleaders' bash was scheduled for the same night as the talent show.

My stomach was suddenly tied up in so many knots

that I knew there was no way anything even resembling lunch was going to make it in there.

"Carla," I breathed, "please tell me I'm just having a nightmare. Say this isn't really happening."

I glanced over and saw that her eyes were also glued to the poster. "I can't believe it," she whispered. "I just can't believe it."

"Well, well, well, if it isn't the big-time talent scouts."

I knew then that this wasn't a nightmare. This was *real*. Wendy Lipton had just sashayed over to me and Carla. She was standing right in front of us, dressed in that ridiculous white cheerleading sweater of hers, grinning from ear to ear. There was a really mean glint in her eyes.

"Welcome to the world of healthy competition," Wendy said coldly.

She turned around and glanced at the poster. "Not bad, huh? I especially like the part that says, 'Tickets, three dollars.' A real bargain, don't you think?"

Wendy let out a loud laugh—a cackle, really. Then she leaned forward so that her face was just a few inches away from mine. "I wonder how many kids are going to want to go to your boring old talent show *now*. As a matter of fact, I wonder if you're even going to get anybody to be in it."

Just then, Kicky came over. "*There* you are, Wendy. I've been looking everywhere for you. I just have to tell you, this entire school is buzzing about the cheerleaders' party. You're an absolute genius. We're going to raise gobs and gobs of money."

Looking over at us and smiling this really fake, sweet smile, she added, "Maybe you two will even want to come."

"Uh, what exactly are you trying to raise money for?" Carla asked. Her voice sounded strained, to say the least.

"Oh, a *very* good cause," she replied earnestly. "We're planning to buy these gorgeous angora sweaters for every one of the cheerleaders."

"That's right," Wendy agreed. "We're going to be the sharpest-looking cheerleading squad in the entire county!"

All of a sudden, Carla began to speak in this really low, really angry voice. She was positively seething.

"How could you?" she said. "Even if you have it in for us, how could you do this to the schoolchildren?"

"Schoolchildren?" Wendy let out this weird, high-pitched laugh. "Let them play tag!"

Kicky joined in then, giggling hysterically.

The two of them laughing like crazed hyenas was drawing kind of a crowd. Quite a few people had noticed the commotion, and they had come over, most of them carrying lunch trays, to see what was going on. I glanced around and saw that there were more than a dozen people standing around, watching this whole scene with as much interest as if they had just been plopped down in front of MTV.

"Don't worry, Carla," Kicky shrieked, nearly doubled over with laughter. "Maybe you'll still get a few people to come to your stupid talent show. Eight . . . maybe nine. . . ."

"Eight or nine!" Wendy cried. "No way! Maybe two or three, if they're *really* lucky!"

I don't know exactly what happened then. I'm not sure I can explain it—or even understand it. All I know is that before I could stop it, before I even knew it was happening, something inside me clicked. All sense of reason, all sense of fairness, fell away. This was *war*.

"We'll get plenty of people to come to our talent show," I said, my voice oddly controlled. "In fact, it's going to be so packed that we'll be selling tickets for Standing Room Only."

"Yeah, right," Kicky said. "And what makes you think *that's* going to happen?"

"I have a perfectly good reason for *knowing* that's what's going to happen," I said in that same eerie voice.

"Oh, really?" Wendy countered, no longer laughing. "What is it?"

The crowd was silent then. I could feel Wendy and Kicky's eyes burning into me. I was aware that beside me, Carla had grown stiff. All the kids who were looking on were strangely silent, too, as if they were also dying to hear what I was about to say.

And then, as if it were actually someone else who was speaking, or at least controlling what words came out of my mouth, I heard myself say, "It just so happens that one of the acts in our talent show is going to be Johnny Rainbow."

"Betsy, have you gone completely *bonkers*?" Carla hissed at me. We had somehow gotten ourselves through the cafeteria line and taken a seat at a corner table, as far away from everybody else as possible. "Have you totally lost your *mind*?"

"Sh-h-h-h," I warned her. "I don't want anybody to overhear you."

"Overhear me? Betsy, we can't do this! You just told a lie—probably the biggest, most outrageous lie of your entire life! What came over you? Are you possessed?"

I looked her straight in the eye. "I don't know what came over me, Carla. All I know is that all of a sudden I felt backed into a corner. I had to come up with *something*."

"Well, I know that, Betsy. But *this*? Starting this crazy story that Johnny Rainbow is going to be in our talent show?"

"I never actually said he was coming." I was squirming in my chair.

"Betsy Crane! I was *there*! And there is only one way that anyone in the entire world could possibly interpret what you said."

"Maybe it's not so crazy," I said hopefully. "Maybe we could call him up on the phone and ask him—"

"Oh, sure. Right," Carla said in a voice dripping with sarcasm. "Just look him up in the telephone book—under 'R,' of course—and call him up and say, 'Oh, hi, Johnny. We just thought that if you weren't doing anything next Saturday night, you'd like to come to our high school and star in our talent show.' " She shook her head hard. "I don't know, Betsy. Maybe you really are possessed."

"I had to do *something*," I repeated, "and that happened to be what popped into my head."

"Okay," Carla said, holding both her hands up. "Let's try looking at this in an entirely different way. What you said just now was so incredibly outrageous that no one in their right mind would ever believe it, right? So we're safe. Word will probably get around that Betsy Crane and Wendy Lipton got into this little argument, and the next thing you know, Betsy said this really silly thing."

She was beginning to calm down. "Of course that's what's going to happen. This whole thing will blow over. In about five seconds flat, everyone will have figured out that you were just . . . exaggerating."

Carla picked up her fork and stabbed the piece of tomato sitting smack in the middle of her salad. "I'm sorry, Betsy. I guess I got a little crazy myself. I mean for a minute there, it actually seemed possible that somebody might *believe* you. . . ."

"Uh, excuse me. Are you, uh, Betsy Crane?"

I looked up and saw that four girls whom I recognized as ninth graders had just come over to our table.

I blinked in confusion, trying to figure out what on earth they could possibly want.

"Yes, that's me."

The girl started to giggle nervously. "Hi. I'm Jill. And, uh, my friends and I were just wondering. . . ."

"Yes?"

Jill took a deep breath. "Is there any chance that maybe we could actually *meet* Johnny Rainbow after the talent show?"

Needless to say, Samantha was about as thrilled with what I had done as Carla was. By three o'clock that afternoon, neither of them was speaking to me.

But I was still speaking to them. At least, I was trying to.

"Look," I said, chasing after them as they walked home from school. They were too furious even to look at me. In fact, they insisted on walking about five feet ahead of me. "It's not my fault! Well, maybe it is my fault. But I was only trying to help!"

Samantha shook her head slowly. Carla just stared straight ahead.

"I don't blame you for being mad at me. Really, I don't. But maybe if the three of us put our heads together, we can come up with some way of dealing with this."

No response.

"I've got it! As soon as I get home, I'm going to call Johnny Rainbow's record company and tell them about this fund-raiser. Maybe if I explain what a good cause it's for and all that, they'd arrange for him to come!''

This time, at least, Samantha looked over at me. Actually, it wasn't a "look" as much as an ice-cold glare.

"Well, I'm going to give it a shot," I mumbled. "It can't hurt to try."

Carla whirled around to face me. "Betsy, there's only one thing you can do."

"What's that?" I asked, blinking.

"You have to tell everybody at school that what you said simply isn't true! That telling Wendy and everybody else that Johnny Rainbow is going to be in our talent show was an out-and-out lie!"

"But . . . but . . . think of all the tickets we'll sell! Isn't that what we intended all along? To do everything we could to raise money for the new playground? Maybe stretching the truth a little isn't so bad. Not if it's for something as worthwhile as this. Haven't you ever heard that expression about how the end justifies the means?"

I really did try to call Johnny Rainbow's record company when I got home from school that afternoon. They suggested that I contact his fan club. When I finally reached them, they told me to write a letter requesting his appearance at a charity event— and to send the organization's financial statements for the past three years.

I was practically in tears when I hung up the phone.

By that point, I didn't know what was making me feel worse: having done such an outlandish thing, or knowing that my two best friends were so angry at me that they could barely bring themselves to talk to me.

I guess that's the end of the Bubble Gum Gang, I thought, on the verge of tears. Those two will never talk to me again. It was the best thing that ever happened to me . . . and now it's over.

Still, I wasn't quite ready to announce to the world that Johnny Rainbow wasn't really going to be in the talent show. In the hour that followed my announcement, I bet fifty people came up to me, wanting to know where they could buy tickets. The way things were going, those kids would be having a new playground practically before they even noticed that the old one was gone.

By the next morning, I was still uncertain about what to do. Part of me could see the point that Carla and Samantha were trying to make. I *had* told a lie. But it seemed like maybe it wasn't such a terrible thing to do when the result of that lie was going to be raising more money than I had ever dared hope for.

I tried to push it out of my mind. For now, I would concentrate on how well ticket sales were doing instead of worrying too much about why.

It turned out that that wasn't very hard to do. The moment I reached homeroom, my teacher, Mr. Arden, came over to me. If I thought he had looked serious that other time, it was nothing compared to the way he looked this time around.

"Betsy," he said, speaking in such a low voice that nobody else could hear, "you are to report to Ms. Trayton's office immediately."

"Why?" I was truly flabbergasted.

"There was another act of vandalism last night. This time, it occurred in the school library."

"But what does that have to do with me?"

Mr. Arden frowned. "Apparently something of yours was found at the scene of the crime. From what I understand, it was some kind of chain, made out of small pieces of paper."

chapter
eight

"The waiting area outside of the principal's office is beginning to feel like my second home," I quipped. I was only trying to make light of a really bad situation. So far, I wasn't having very much luck.

There we were again, all three of us, huddled together in our chairs in the corner of the office, watching the school secretaries talk on the phone and file and type. Just like last time. Only this time, things were even worse, for two very good reasons.

The first one was the bubble gum chain, the first solid piece of evidence that had been found at the scenes of the three acts of vandalism. If we had felt we had some explaining to do last time, that was nothing compared to the fancy footwork we were going to have to do now.

The second reason that this situation was even worse than last time was that this time around, Carla and Samantha were still angry at me about the Johnny Rainbow business. So much for moral support.

"Girls?" Ms. Trayton said coldly, coming out of her office. "Please come in."

We filed in, taking the exact same seats as last time. Instant replay. My stomach, meanwhile, was also feeling pretty much the same as last time. And that, I'm afraid, was not good.

The school principal sat down behind her desk, folding her hands in front of her. "In case you haven't heard, there's been another act of vandalism committed in our school. This is the third time in the past eight days.

"This time, it was in the school library. Mr. Pease's office, in fact." She let out a long, deep sigh. "At least this time there was no shaving cream involved. That would have been an awful mess, since there's carpeting everywhere in the library."

"W-what happened?" I asked.

She looked at me oddly. It only took me a second to figure out that the reason for her surprise was that at the moment we were her number-one suspects. It was only natural that she would expect us to know already.

"Sawdust," she replied. "Sawdust, everywhere. All over Mr. Pease's desk, inside the file cabinets, even in his desktop computer. I just hope the computer company we leased it from has a way of dealing with it. Our theory is that the sawdust was taken from the woodworking shop, where there's a big bin filled with it, waiting to be recycled. Aside from that, Mr. Pease's papers were pulled out of their files and strewn about everywhere.'' Shaking her head, she added, ''It's going to take him *weeks* to sort through it all.''

Ms. Trayton reached into the top drawer of her desk. ''And lying in one corner—as if it had been dropped accidentally—we found this.''

I wasn't at all surprised to see her pull the bubble gum wrapper chain—*my* bubble gum wrapper chain— out of her top drawer. I could feel myself shrinking lower and lower into my chair. I could also feel Samantha and Carla, sitting on either side of me, growing even more tense.

''This is yours, I presume?''

She asked the question of all three of us, but I took it upon myself to answer.

''Actually, that's mine,'' I said. My voice sounded kind of like a frog's. A frog who happened to be very, very nervous. ''I, uh, made it out of bubble gum wrappers.''

''So I understand. According to Mr. Homer, you showed this to your English class last week, as part of a presentation you were giving on friendship.''

She paused, studying the bubble gum wrapper chain. I wondered if I were ever going to get it back. I wondered if, after this, I would ever even *want* it back.

''So the three of you belong to some sort of secret club, is that it?''

''It's not a secret,'' Carla insisted.

At the same time, Samantha said, ''It's not a club.''

''It's really just a name we came up with,'' I explained. "Back at the beginning of the school year, the three of us became friends. We decided that one of the things we wanted to do together was try to solve mysteries."

"Mysteries? You intend to solve mysteries?" Ms. Trayton looked skeptical.

"We already have," Carla piped up. "We solved the puzzle behind a haunted house, and we investigated a shoplifting incident over at the mall. We even helped Mr. Langtree, Samantha's father, find out which one of his employees was selling company secrets."

The principal did not look impressed. "Well, girls, it looks as if we have one more mystery on our hands. We're not calling in the police, but that doesn't mean we don't intend to get to the bottom of it ourselves. And from where I sit, it looks as if all the evidence points in one direction."

"Ms. Trayton, may we please have a chance to explain?" I pleaded.

"Of course."

"Okay. First of all, I just want to say that none of us had anything to do with any of this. Mr. James was willing to back us up last time, but this time it turns out we're not quite as lucky. We don't have anybody to back up our story. That's why you've simply got to believe us!"

I could see I wasn't making much headway. Her expression didn't change a bit.

"As for the bubble gum wrapper chain, it's something I carry around all the time. I keep it in my book bag. This one, right here.'' I held up the green canvas bag that had been lying at my feet, as if to prove to her how honest I was. "I noticed a couple of days ago that the chain was missing. At first, I just figured I'd lost it somehow. Then I got so caught up in the talent show and everything else that I forgot all about it.''

I swallowed hard. "Ms. Trayton, this whole thing is a big mistake. I can't explain how my bubble gum wrapper chain ended up in Mr. Pease's office. But I do know that I didn't have anything to do with it getting there.''

"Betsy's telling the truth," Samantha insisted. "I'm sure if you call her mother, she'll tell you that she was at home all last evening. That *is* when the vandals broke into Mr. Pease's office, isn't it?''

"Actually, we can't be sure. For all we know, the incident could have occurred early this morning.''

"Besides," I said quietly, "I wasn't at home for the whole evening. I took a long walk, all by myself. I really wanted to do some thinking without anybody else around.''

"Girls, given the evidence," Ms. Trayton said, sounding exasperated, "I'm afraid I have to conclude that it was the three of you who were responsible—''

"Excuse me, Ms. Trayton," Carla said suddenly. "I just had an idea.''

The principal looked kind of annoyed at having been interrupted. But there was a firmness—and,

oddly enough, a kind of optimism—in Carla's voice.
I know I heard it. And Ms. Trayton seemed to as
well.

"Yes, Carla? What is it?"

"We were saying before that the three of us have
kind of a hobby, solving mysteries. And that so far,
we have a pretty good track record."

"So you say. What about it?"

Carla took a deep breath. "Ms. Trayton, before
you make up your mind that it's the Bubble Gum Gang
that's responsible for all this awful vandalism, do you
think maybe you could let us try to solve this mystery
ourselves?"

Samantha brightened. "That's a wonderful idea!
Please let us, Ms. Trayton. We know we're innocent.
All we want is the chance to prove it."

I must admit, I was kind of taken aback. Sure, we
had tackled mysteries before. And Carla was right; it
was turning out that we were pretty good at it. But
attempting to solve one in order to clear our own
names? That was a new twist!

But even though the idea sounded a little bit wacky
at first, it didn't take me long to see that it was, in
fact, a good idea. A great idea, in fact.

I really had faith that if anybody could solve this
mystery, it was the Bubble Gum Gang.

"How much time are you girls asking for?" Ms.
Trayton said. She still sounded as if she had her
doubts. But at least she hadn't refused. At least, not
yet.

Carla looked at me and Samantha. "Gosh, I don't know. A day? Two days? Three days? What do you think?"

Sam and I never did get a chance to answer.

"I'll give you girls forty-eight hours to solve this mystery," Ms. Trayton said. "If you can prove that someone other than the three of you is behind this, then I will owe you all an apology."

One at a time, she looked at each of us, first Samantha, then Carla, then me.

"But if you can't," she said earnestly, her eyes still fixed on me, "I'm going to have to go along with my initial conclusion. I'll have to act on the assumption that the owners of the bubble gum wrapper chain are the vandals."

"Forty-eight hours!" I groaned. "How on *earth* are we ever going to solve this mystery in forty-eight hours?"

"We've got to," Carla replied. "We don't have a choice. It's that, or else . . . well, I'm not even going to *think* about the 'or else.' "

Of the three of us, Samantha was the most calm. "Look, you two. There's no need to panic. Forty-eight hours is plenty of time. We might not even need that long. Not if we can zoom right in on this."

"Zoom in?" I repeated, looking at her. "And h< may I ask, do you propose we accomplish this zc ing?"

We were sitting in an empty classroom right

the hall from the school library, perched on top of
desks, planning our strategy. We had just come out
of Ms. Trayton's office. Instead of feeling relieved,
however, I felt as if the hardest part had just begun.
In the past, solving mysteries had always had an ele-
ment of excitement, adventure . . . maybe even fun.
Even during the scariest parts, I always knew I could
turn back if I wanted to.

This time, there would be no turning back. The
stakes were much too high.

Even in that darkest hour, however, there was a tiny
glimmer of hope, an itsy-bitsy sliver of silver lining
in the rain cloud. At least the other members of the
Bubble Gum Gang were talking to me again. For now,
the Johnny Rainbow incident had been put on a back
burner. Not much, I know, given what we were all
going through. But it was *something*.

"Okay," I said, trying to sound optimistic. "Let's
decide what we're going to do first. Any ideas?"

Samantha shrugged. "I'd say that's pretty clear. Ms.
Trayton gave us permission to look around Mr. Pease's
ʿfice, just as long as we don't touch anything. That's
ʾest bet. If that doesn't work, our next step is to try
ʿto people. Maybe we'll get lucky and find some-
knows something—anything."

nodding. "Good thinking. Your idea of
ʾt for the scene of the crime sounds

tone of her voice, and the telltale
ı her cheeks, that she was starting

to get into this. I wondered if the fact that she was trying to solve this mystery for her own sake could be making this whole thing even more of an adventure for her.

But this didn't seem the time to ask.

"Okay, then. It's settled. The scene of the crime is where we start. Carla and I are free fifth period. Why don't we start then?" The idea of skipping lunch—especially the part about sitting in a room full of people, some of them on my Top Ten Cheerleaders to Avoid list—sounded pretty good to me. "How about you, Sam? Can you get out of class then?"

She nodded. "I'll just explain to my teacher that this is an emergency."

"Great." I rubbed my hands together. "Now, what exactly are we going to be looking for?"

"Physical evidence," Samantha replied. "Clues. Anything we can find that will help lead us to the real vandals."

"Maybe we can dust for fingerprints," Carla suggested.

I let out a little gasp. "I had no idea you knew how to do that!"

"I don't. But that's where the F.B.I. always starts. In the movies, anyway."

"Really, Carla," I said, "I don't think that—"

"Wait a minute," Samantha interrupted. "That's not as outrageous as it sounds."

I just looked at her. "Not you, too, Sam. I think you've been reading too much Dick Tracy."

"No, no, not the part about fingerprints." Samantha was starting to sound exasperated. "What I meant was, I think it's a good idea to look for tiny clues. The kind of things that less-experienced investigators would probably miss."

She didn't know it, but she had just given me an idea.

"Okay, tell you what," I said, grabbing my stuff and hopping off the desk. "I'll meet you at the library at the beginning of fifth period. But before I do, there's a special mission I have to carry out."

"A special mission?" Samantha asked, her eyebrows shooting up.

"It sounds like there's *another* mystery underfoot," added Carla.

I just laughed.

chapter
nine

"I know in my head that it's a good idea to get going on this as soon as we can," Carla said as she and Samantha and I met outside the cafeteria later that same day, just as fifth period was beginning. "But in my heart, I'm scared stiff."

"Why?" Samantha asked in a gentle voice. "Are you afraid of what we might find?"

Carla made a face. "I'm afraid of what we might *not* find."

As I followed them down the second-floor corridor toward the library, I longed to say something comforting to her.

Don't worry, Carla, I wanted to say to her in a hearty voice. You're talking about the Bubble Gum Gang here. We've never been stumped yet.

But the words just wouldn't come out. That was mainly because, deep down, I was feeling the same way she was feeling.

What if we *didn't* find anything? What if all the

evidence continued to point to us . . . and we couldn't prove our innocence? As the three of us shuffled into the library, our footsteps suddenly silenced by the thick blue carpeting, that possibility loomed above us like an ugly, gray rain cloud.

"Has anybody besides Ms. Trayton and Mr. Pease been in here?" I asked as we lingered outside the school librarian's office, still trying to muster up the courage to go in.

Samantha shook her head. "According to Mr. James, the custodian, no one's touched a thing. Ms. Trayton felt it was best to leave everything exactly as it was found this morning until this whole thing is cleared up."

"Good." I nodded. "Well, then, are you ready?"

Carla shrugged. "Ready as we'll ever be, I guess."

When we walked in, Carla let out a yelp. Samantha cried, "Oh, my gosh!"

I, meanwhile, let out a loud gasp. I guess I hadn't known what to expect—but certainly not this. Mr. Pease's office was in shambles. There were three tall, metal file cabinets pushed up against the back wall, and from the way that small room looked, every one of them had been dumped onto the floor. There were papers everywhere—still in their file folders, but piled up haphazardly. Ms. Trayton was right; from the looks of things, it really was going to take him ages to put everything back where it belonged.

Then there was the sawdust. Ms. Trayton hadn't

been exaggerating when she said it was everywhere. It looked as if it had snowed. *Brown* snow.

At least I hadn't come totally unprepared. In addition to bringing a small notebook—for writing down clues, of course—I had made a stop at the science lab between second and third periods. That was my "special mission": to borrow a magnifying glass. I thought it was a great idea; after all, it always seemed to work for Sherlock Holmes. But the moment I brought it out of my green canvas book bag, both Carla and Samantha burst out laughing.

"What?" I demanded, blinking hard. "What's so funny?"

"I'm sorry, Betsy," Sam said between giggles. "It's just that you look like something out of a movie."

"I think you've been watching too many old detective films on TV on Saturday afternoons," Carla said with a chuckle.

"All right, all right," I grumbled, slipping it back into my book bag. "Maybe I *am* overdoing this—just a little."

For the next half hour, the three of us covered every base. We wanted to be careful not to disturb anything, but since most of Mr. Pease's drawers and files had been emptied onto the floor, that wasn't very difficult. We peered into the open drawers. We peeked under the piles of paper strewn in messy heaps across his desk. We even went through his trash basket, hoping to find something . . . anything. But that had been emptied by Mr. James some time the night before, before the vandals had gotten inside the room. There wasn't even a scrap of paper in there, much less any clues.

I was beginning to think all this was a waste of time. The clock was ticking, fifth period was getting to be old news, and I didn't have the slightest idea where to go. I guess I had been hoping that some big fat clue was going to hit us in the face. Like maybe the real vandals would have left something behind . . . something like a library card with one of their names on it. No such luck.

I was telling myself that that kind of thing only happens in the movies when I remembered that it was exactly what had happened here. Except that instead of a library card, the clue had been a paper chain made out of bubble gum wrappers. And that instead of leading to the real vandals, all it did was point the finger at three innocent bystanders—whom, it appeared, somebody was trying to frame.

"All right," I finally said, sinking onto the floor. "We've only got a few minutes left before the bell rings. We're not getting very far with this. Why don't we take a couple of minutes to review everything we know so far?"

I sat cross-legged, leaning against the wall. I hated to admit it, even to myself, but I was beginning to think we weren't going to get anywhere with this case.

"Okay," Sam agreed. "Let's put it all down on paper."

She leaned against Mr. Pease's desk. Carla, meanwhile, dropped into his desk chair. I had to look up in order to see them, as if I were at the bottom of a deep hole. Somehow, that went along perfectly with the way I was feeling.

"I'll just get out a notebook. . . ." I stuck my hand into my book bag. Since I was trying to be methodical, writing all our clues down in my little notebook made perfect sense. Maybe, just maybe, I was thinking, if I see everything written down, it will all somehow click into place.

"First of all, we know that whoever did this did it after Mr. James cleaned up in here last night."

"Right," Carla agreed. "The empty trash basket tells us that."

"Which means the incident occurred either very late last night or—what's even more likely—very early this morning."

Samantha sighed. "All that tells us is that the vandals go to this school, and that, if they were spotted, they didn't look at all suspicious. And because of the size of the footprints that were found in the mud near Mr. Homer's house when his car was smeared with shaving cream, we already knew that."

"Just trying to be thorough," I said with a shrug. "Okay. So we're still working under the theory that the vandals are most likely students. As far as we know, no one spotted anyone here early this morning, so we don't have any suspects. . . ."

"Unless," Carla said, her face lighting up, "we can think of the sawdust as a clue."

"The sawdust?" I repeated, not quite getting it.

"Right!" She was growing excited. "The sawdust was stored in the woodworking shop, right? So there's a good chance that whoever did this was also taking a woodworking class. . . ."

"Are you thinking of anyone in particular?" I asked.

She folded her arms across her chest. "I know of two gentlemen who seem to have been quite amused by the story of the Bubble Gum Gang, two boys from our English class, if you get my drift. It's possible that—"

"Wait a minute," Samantha interrupted. "Don't get carried away. If we're talking about kids who are taking woodworking, we're talking about a very large percentage of the students in this school. Maybe we can't keep ourselves from having our suspicions, but without anything more than that to go on, we can't very well start making accusations." She sighed. "If only we had another clue."

I had to agree. Maybe we had our suspicions, but we had no real evidence. Carla realized that, too; the way her face fell was proof. I stared at my notebook. There wasn't much written in it. And what was written there wasn't getting any of us anywhere.

I swallowed hard. "Look, I hate to be the one to say this, but it looks as if we might have hit a dead end. We've only got about five minutes left before the period ends, and to be perfectly honest, I don't know where to go from here.''

"What about asking people if they saw anyone or anything suspicious?'' Samantha asked softly. "Wasn't that supposed to be step two?''

"Yes . . . but to tell you the truth, I wouldn't know where to begin,'' I replied with a shrug.

"I guess you've got a point,'' Sam said. "Besides, the whole school is talking about this. If anyone had seen anything, I'm sure it would have been reported to the principal by now.''

Carla's face looked pale. "Maybe . . . maybe the Bubble Gum Gang has finally met up with a case it can't solve.''

"Maybe,'' I said, my voice hoarse. "Too bad the people we were trying to solve it for was *us*.''

None of us felt like talking after that. We were all quiet for a long time. It was Samantha who finally got up off the edge of Mr. Pease's desk and started walking slowly to the door. I could see that we really had hit that dead end. I grabbed the strap of my book bag and slid it toward me, along the carpet, so I could put my notebook away.

"I know we still have time left to try to solve this case,'' Sam said, "since Ms. Trayton did give us forty-eight hours and all. But maybe we should just go tell her that—''

"Wait a minute,'' I said.

As I was pulling my book bag toward me, the magnifying glass had slipped out. It was lying on the rug right next to me. I had completely forgotten about it. But as I glanced over at it, not really paying all that much attention, I noticed that its silver metal rim was acting like a picture frame—a picture frame that was highlighting something in a way it hadn't been highlighted before.

"Hold on just a second," I said again, leaning forward to get a better look. And then, in a voice I barely recognized as my own, I cried, "Oh, my *goodness*!"

"What? What?" Within seconds Carla and Samantha were kneeling on the floor, peering at the magnifying glass, trying to see what I had seen.

Carla was frowning. "I don't see anything. What is it, Betsy? Sam, do you see anything?"

"Yes," Samantha breathed. "I see it, too. Betsy Crane, you are an absolute genius. Even better than that, you are without doubt the best sleuth that has ever walked the face of this earth!"

"What is everybody seeing that I'm not seeing?" Carla demanded. "Will somebody please tell me what's going on?"

I was grinning from ear to ear. "Look through the magnifying glass," I instructed her. "Tell me what you see."

Carla leaned forward so that her nose was practically touching the glass. "I see . . . I see a blue rug. A blue rug made out of fibers that have been blown up to look really huge." She screwed up her face as she looked even more closely. "I must say, it's not a very *clean* rug. It's covered with little white threads."

"What kind of little white threads?" I looked over at Samantha. She, too, was grinning.

"I don't know," Carla said. "Fuzzy white threads. That's funny, I can't imagine Mr. Pease wearing anything like that."

All of a sudden, she looked as if she had been hit by a bolt of lightning. Understanding swept over her face like a gust of wind. Her eyes grew bright. Within a fraction of a second, she was also grinning, just like Sam and me.

"Mr. Pease doesn't wear clothes with fuzzy white threads on them, and he's the only one who's supposed to come in here. But I know two people who *do* wear clothes with fuzzy white threads."

"With black and orange trim," Samantha added.

"And tigers," I said, laughing. "Don't forget the tigers."

"I can't believe that Wendy and Kicky would actually do this," Carla cried, growing serious. "And that they would actually try to frame *us* by putting our bubble gum chain at the scene of the crime!"

"A *stolen* bubble gum chain, no less," Samantha pointed out. "They must have slipped it out of your book bag, Betsy, when you weren't looking."

"I guess they think they're pretty smart," I said. "But *we're* even smarter!"

I felt a million miles tall as I tucked the magnifying

glass—the wonderful, stupendous magnifying glass—
back into my book bag.

"Do you think Ms. Trayton is in her office?" I
asked Carla and Samantha. "Let's go see if we can
find her."

"Back to the principal's office," Carla quipped.
"Our home away from home."

"It's a funny thing," I commented, picking up my
book bag and slinging it over my shoulder. "This is
one time I don't mind going there at all."

So there we were again, sitting in the principal's
office. Only this time, it really was different. This
time, we were the ones doing most of the talking.

This time, Ms. Trayton believed us.

"Well, girls," she said, her voice softer and kinder
than I had ever before heard it, "I can see I owe all
of you an apology."

"The main thing," Samantha said, "is for justice
to be done."

"That's right," Carla agreed. Then, more to herself than to anyone else, she added, "I can hardly
wait to hear what Wendy and Kicky have to say for
themselves."

Within ten minutes, none other than those two
"themselves" were also sitting in Ms. Trayton's office. Now, suddenly, it was *their* turn to do some
explaining.

But before they had a chance to tell the principal
their story, Ms. Trayton received an important tele-

phone call. She went into another office to talk in private. That left the five of us—Wendy, Kicky, plus the Bubble Gum Gang—alone.

"Well, well, well," Carla said the moment Ms. Trayton left the room, closing the door behind her. "We meet again."

"We're going to prove that you're lying," Wendy countered. "No matter what you've been telling Ms. Trayton, we can prove that you're making it up."

"It's a little late for that," I said, not without satisfaction. "Not only have we already proved to Ms. Trayton that you two are responsible for all three acts of vandalism that have occurred during the past couple of weeks, but also that you were trying to make it look as if we were responsible."

"You . . . you haven't heard the last of this!" Wendy spat out her words. "I'll tell my parents. I'll call the local newspapers. I'll . . . I'll. . . ."

"Let it go, Wendy. It's over."

Kicky had spoken in such a quiet voice that it took me a second or two to realize that she had spoken at all. I glanced over at her and saw that she was slouched way down in her chair, with her shoulders slumped and her head down, studying the floor. When she finally did look up at us, her eyes were filled with tears.

"It's too late to make excuses," Kicky said in that same low voice. "I think we'd better just own up to it before we get ourselves into any more trouble."

"But . . . but . . . but. . . ."

By this point, nobody was interested in listening to Wendy's excuses. Instead, I asked Kicky, "Why did you do it?"

Kicky, still looking miserable, simply said, "It was all Wendy's idea."

"It was *not*!" Wendy burst out. "If you think you're going to get away with blaming it all on me—"

"Wendy!" Kicky sounded angry for the first time. "Will you please give it up?"

Wendy stuck her chin up in the air. "All right, I admit it. It was my idea. And it was a brilliant idea. If you three hadn't gone poking around in Mr. Pease's office, the whole thing would have been perfect."

"But why?" Samantha demanded, sounding as if she couldn't quite believe what she was hearing. "Why did you do it, Wendy?"

The blond cheerleader smiled coldly. "Because I thought it was about time that the rest of the school found out the truth about you."

"What is that supposed to mean?" Carla cried.

"The three of you go around acting like such do-gooders. Little Mary Sunshines, each one of you." Wendy's eyes had narrowed into thin slits. "Giving corny speeches about how you go around calling yourselves the Bubble Gum Gang. Trying to raise money for some silly playground just so everybody would think you were important."

"But that's not why we—" I protested.

"I was certain that, in the end, justice would pre-vail," Wendy concluded. "Sure, it meant fighting dirty. But the way I see it, the end always justifies the means."

That expression. There was something about it. . . . I could remember somebody using it not long before, only in an entirely different context.

The wheels inside my brain were turning. Slowly, gradually, through the fog. . . .

And then I remembered. Of course. That "somebody" had been me.

The Johnny Rainbow business. The way I had started a rumor, one that wasn't even close to being true. No matter how you looked at it, I had lied. And I had tried to convince myself that what I had done wasn't so bad because it was all for such a good cause. Because Wendy and Kicky had backed me into a corner. Because "the end justifies the means."

Yet that was precisely what Wendy had done. She had tried to frame us. In leaving the bubble gum chain in Mr. Pease's office, by spraying shaving cream all over the classroom that everybody knew we were using, she had made it look like we were the vandals. She, too, had lied.

And through it all, she had been telling herself that the end justified the means. She convinced herself that doing whatever you had to do to get what you wanted was perfectly acceptable—no matter how many lies were told, no matter who got hurt along the way—as long as the "end" was something you considered important.

The moment I understood what I had done, I also understood exactly what I had to do about it.

"Hey, Carla? Sam?" All of a sudden, I couldn't wait to tell them. But at that moment Ms. Trayton came back into her office.

"I'm sorry about the interruption," she said, sitting down behind her desk. "But now that I've finished with that telephone call, I'm all ears."

This time, the principal barely looked at me or Samantha or Carla.

"Wendy," she said, turning her attention toward her, "why don't we begin with you?"

chapter
ten

If this is what it feels like to be a star, I was thinking, I'll try out for the role of ticket seller any day.

It was first thing Monday morning, and I was sitting in the main office. In just five minutes, Ms. Trayton would be getting on the loudspeaker to make the usual announcements that always came blasting into each and every classroom during homeroom.

Only this time, when she was finished, it would be my turn. And that was why the butterflies were back. From what was going on in my stomach, I figured they were playing a game of basketball or field hockey or something.

This, I had decided, was the best way to undo what I had already done. The Friday before, right after the meeting between one school principal, two cheerleaders, and three Bubble Gum Gang members, Carla and Samantha and I had made a beeline for YoYo's Yogurt. We deserved to celebrate, Carla insisted, since we had just solved another mystery—and cleared our own names to boot.

There, in addition to consuming more delicious frozen yogurt than most people would ever think possible, given the fact that there are only three of us, we talked. We talked for almost two hours, in fact. Sam and Carla were thrilled that I had finally realized that I had to come clean about the Johnny Rainbow business.

That's what I was doing in the main office. I had never been on the radio, but I suspected that it didn't feel that different from stepping up to the microphone that was used to make the morning announcements. Every time I thought of my voice echoing through the halls of good old Hanover Junior High, I felt dizzy. But somehow, I knew, I was going to have to do it.

As I was wondering for the eight millionth time exactly where I was ever going to get the courage to carry this off, the answer sauntered over and stood right in front of me.

"Guess who?" cried Carla, leaping into the office.

Samantha wasn't far behind. "Hi, Betsy. Are you still in one piece?"

"What are you two doing here?" I exclaimed.

Carla just looked at me funny. "You didn't think we'd let you go through this alone, did you?"

"No way," Samantha replied, with a teasing smile. "Not as long as you've got the Bubble Gum Gang on your side."

I felt like crying. But there wasn't time. Ms. Trayton came out of her office and picked up the microphone. Looking over in my direction, she said, "It's time, Betsy."

I gulped. The idea of actually standing up, of leaving the safety of that chair, seemed like an impossibility.

And then Samantha came over to me. In a soft voice, she said, "Come on, Betsy. We're right here."

"Sure, Betsy," Carla said heartily. "You know that old show biz expression: break a leg."

And that was how I overcame my shyness enough to stand up and go over to the microphone. After Ms. Trayton made a few announcements, something about the school newspaper and something else about a gymnastics meet being canceled, she looked over at me and smiled encouragingly.

"And now," she said, "we'll be hearing from Betsy Crane, the organizer of the talent show that's being held this weekend to raise money for a new playground at the elementary school."

She handed me the microphone.

Samantha and Carla were standing opposite me, nodding and grinning. I took a deep breath. It was time to put things right.

"Uh, hello," I said. My voice sounded highpitched, not the way I usually sound at all. I cleared my throat. "Uh . . ." I began once again.

And then, from out of nowhere, I really did get the courage to go on. The words came gushing out all at once. And as I heard the sound of my own voice filling the school, instead of feeling nervous and scared, I felt relieved that, finally, the lying was over.

"There's been a rumor around school," I said, "that Johnny Rainbow is going to be appearing at the talent show this weekend. I must admit that I was actually the one who started that rumor, and I apologize. Now, I want to make sure that everybody understands that Johnny Rainbow is *not* going to be in the talent show. We will have some great acts—singers and dancers and magicians and all kinds of great entertainers—but not Johnny Rainbow."

To tell you the truth, that was pretty much all I had intended to say. But now that I was there, the words kept pouring out of me.

"You know, when I first started working on this fund-raising project, I wanted it to succeed so badly that I was ready to do anything. All I could think of was those kids not having a playground. Nothing else seemed to matter.

"But what's even more important to me is having learned a real lesson. I understand now that lying is no way to achieve anything, no matter how noble you might believe your cause to be. Sure, it's easy to say that the end justifies the means. But if you can't get what you want honestly, then it's not worth getting at all.

"Now if there's anybody who's already bought a ticket and wants to get his or her money back, there won't be any problem. But I hope you'll come anyway. Maybe I can't deliver Johnny Rainbow next Saturday night, but I can certainly give you a really fun evening chockful of local talent.''

I handed the microphone back to Ms. Trayton. I can't remember having ever felt that relieved before—and having the speech over with was only a small part of it.

"Well," I said, turning to Samantha and Carla, "how did I do?"

"You were great!" Carla cried, reaching over and hugging me. "You just gave the performance of a lifetime."

"We're really proud of you," Samantha added.

Sam and Carla weren't the only ones who had something to say. After she finished up with a few more announcements, Ms. Trayton came over to me.

"Betsy," she said, "you just did a very brave thing. I admire you for coming forward and telling the truth. I hope your talent show is a great success."

As the three of us filed into the hallway, the corridors were already filling up. Homeroom was over. Everybody was rushing to first-period class. But for once, Sam and Carla and I were taking our time.

"You know," I said thoughtfully, "I really do think that show is going to be a real hit. We've got some great acts, and we've all been putting so much effort into the posters and the publicity and everything."

"I think so, too," Samantha agreed. "We're going to raise lots of money for the playground. We don't need Johnny Rainbow!"

Carla laughed. "And it certainly won't hurt that

Ms. Trayton made Wendy and Kicky cancel that cheerleaders' party. Talk about justice being served!''

"There's one more thing I'm really glad about, too," I added shyly.

"What's that?" asked Carla and Sam.

"That you two aren't mad at me anymore. When I think about how angry you got when I told that lie about Johnny Rainbow. . . ." I shuddered. "I was really afraid that the Bubble Gum Gang was going to fall apart."

"Never!" Samantha cried.

"No way!" Carla insisted. "Look, Betsy, it's okay if we get mad at each other. We're three different people, so we can't expect to see eye-to-eye on everything. What really matters is whether or not we can work out those differences. Whether we can find a way to live with the parts of one another that aren't perfect, as well as the really great things."

"If anything," Samantha said, "I'd say that after this, the Bubble Gum Gang is stronger than ever. After all, we've proven that we can go through some rough times and still survive."

"Yeah," Carla said. "You don't think a few little disagreements are going to get in the way of our friendship, do you?"

I laughed. And once again, I thanked my lucky stars—or whatever it was that was responsible for putting me together with such great pals.

"There's just one thing," I said, pausing outside

Mr. Homer's classroom, knowing we had just a few seconds before the bell rang.

"What's that?" Sam asked.

"The next time we solve a mystery, let's make sure it's not *our* necks we're trying to save!"

Poor Mr. Homer never did figure out why all three of us had such a hard time keeping a straight face that day.